WISE CHILD

Also by Monica Furlong

JUNIPER

COLMAN

WISE CHILD

MONICA FURLONG

Random House ⌂ New York

Text copyright © 1987 by Monica Furlong.
Jacket illustration copyright © 1987 by Leo and Diane Dillon.
All rights reserved under International and Pan-American Copyright Conventions.
Published in the United States by Random House Children's Books, a division of
Random House, Inc., New York, and simultaneously in Canada by Random House of
Canada Limited, Toronto. Originally published in Great Britain by Victor Gollancz Ltd.
and in the United States as a Borzoi Book by Alfred A. Knopf, an imprint of Random
House Children's Books, a division of Random House, Inc., in 1987.

www.randomhouse.com/teens

Library of Congress Cataloging-in-Publication Data
Furlong, Monica. Wise Child.
SUMMARY: Abandoned by both her parents, nine-year-old Wise Child goes to live with the
witch woman Juniper, who begins to train her in the ways of herbs and magic.
ISBN 0-394-89105-8 (trade) — ISBN 0-394-99105-2 (lib. bdg.) —
ISBN 0-394-82598-5 (pbk.)
[1. Witchcraft—Fiction.] I. Title.
PZ7.F96638Wi 1987 [Fic] 87-3063

Printed in the United States of America
11 10 9 8 7 6 5 4 3 2

RANDOM HOUSE and colophon are registered trademarks of Random House, Inc.

To my grandmother, Neni,
and to Nina Coltart,
with gratitude and love

CONTENTS

WISE CHILD

1

Juniper

JUNIPER was different from us. In the first place she came from another country—Cornwall—and although she spoke our language perfectly, apart from the *p*'s, which no one but us could pronounce properly, she looked different. She was taller, darker skinned, and although she had black hair as Finbar and I did, she did not have our bright-blue eyes. Her eyes were a soft, dark color, brooding and quiet.

Then again, she did not live as our women lived. She was what in our language was called a *cailleach*—it meant a single woman, but more than a single woman, one who had something uncanny about her. In our village the women were the wives of farm workers, of sailors, of fishermen, with swarms of children tumbling over their doorsteps. The few who were unmarried lived at home and looked after their parents. No woman lived alone, as Juniper did.

Juniper lived away from the village, high up in a white stone house set on a sort of inland cliff that looked as if, a few yards from the front of her garden, the ground had suddenly split open. Behind her house was a great meadow covered in spring and summer with flowers. Beyond that, as I was one day to learn, was a moor, fragrant with mint and asphodel and bog myrtle, and beyond that again blue mountains. At night up there the stars seemed very close, and by day you felt as if you were on the roof of the world.

At the front of her house was a winding path that led down to the village; there were sheep tracks and caves in the red wall of the cliff. The front of her house looked toward the village and the back of it onto her herb garden and the moor.

The most important thing that separated Juniper from the rest of us was that she did magic. When we called her a *cailleach,* what we really meant was that she was a witch, a sorceress, probably in the pay of the Devil. Proof was that she did not come to Mass on Sundays, when the priest held aloft the bread and the wine. She came to the village when people were desperate and did not care anymore if Fillan Priest disapproved of them. When a man whose wife had labored for hours in vain could not stand it any longer, when someone was near to death after an accident, when a child was delirious with fever, when a woman had an evil spirit, they sent for Juniper; and whatever she did (and no two people ever agreed about what she did), as often as not the patient recovered. It did not seem to make us grateful; on the contrary, it only increased our feeling that she was a witch.

I was really frightened of her as a tiny child. Mothers in our village used to threaten their children, "I'll give you to Juniper if you are naughty." I wonder if Maeve so threatened me. Of course, Juniper wasn't the witch's real name. Like so many in our village she was called by a nickname—in this case because the plant juniper was a favorite remedy of hers. It was easy enough for people like us to get hold of—we could go and get it up on the mountain, and in a village where many were very poor, it was cheap medicine for many ailments.

MY EARLIEST MEMORY of Juniper was when I was a little child of three or four standing in the village street while my grandmother chatted with a group of neighbors. Suddenly a silence came upon us as Juniper passed, with a friendly word to the women and a smile for me that I did not return. I buried my face in my grandmother's skirt—I can smell the fusty, old-woman smell now—and did not breathe again until the tall figure had passed on her way. My grandmother had put her hand on my head to reassure me, but with childish logic I reasoned that she would not do that if Juniper were not dangerous.

THE FIRST TIME that Juniper and I had anything you could really call a conversation was when I was about five. I spent a lot of time with my cousins because my mother, a woman so beautiful that she was known as Maeve the Fair, had left by then, and my grandmother was getting too old to care for me all the time. (My father, Finbar, was usually away at sea, sailing that angry triangle between Wales and Dalriada and Ireland. Sometimes too he sailed to Cornwall or to Brittany, and brought back tin or silver ore or copper or finely wrought armor or salt.)

I was younger than all but the youngest of my cousins,

and an only child who had tantrums when she did not get
her own way. Looking back, I am amazed at how patient
they were with me, especially as, at least at the beginning,
I had more to eat and nicer clothes than they had. Like
Juniper and many others, I was not called by my proper
name, but by a teasing word that you would translate into
English as "Wise Child." This was not a compliment—it
was a word for children who used long words, as I often did,
or who had big eyes, or who seemed somehow old beyond
their years. I did not mind it, since I admired my cousins so
much and felt loved by them and it was such fun to be
among them and petted by them.

It was an autumn day, golden and still. We had gone to
the shore and played there, Conor and Domnall, Seumas
and Fingal, Bride, Morag, Mairi, Colman, and me. Then,
with big baskets, we had wandered until we found the
fields where the blackberries grew thickly, huge walls of
bramble encrusted with luscious hulls like red and black
thimbles. I did not pick very quickly, because I stopped
so often to eat the fruit, but in the end I filled a small
basket.

On the way home I got tired. It was getting toward dark,
it was cold and misty, and the scratches on my arms and
legs, which had not bothered me before, began to hurt. The
basket felt heavy, and I wanted to be carried. Conor carried
me for a long way on his back, and Colman, always a friend
to me, though not much bigger than I was myself, carried
my basket, but in the end they too were tired, and Conor set
me down on the track and Colman returned my basket.

"Walk!" said Conor.

I had loved riding on Conor's broad back, and I did not

want to walk. I sulked, I dragged behind while the others waited for me, and finally I sat down on the ground, thinking this would force Conor to carry me again.

"Very well," said Conor. "We will go on without you."

"The *tarans* may get you," said Mairi, who had always had a spiteful streak. "Or the people of the Sidh." The *tarans* were the ghosts of unbaptized babies who were said to snatch children away, and the people of the Sidh were the fairies, the Shining Ones.

To my amazement they all walked off and left me sitting there—they were sick to death of my temperamental outbursts—only Colman looking uncertainly back over his shoulder. I could see their white and brown smocks growing fainter as they crossed one field and passed into another, and finally they were gone. The darkness was edging the bushes and gently nudging its way into the corners of the fields, and the sky was a dim blue like the eye of an angry old man. I was shocked at their desertion.

It did not occur to me to get up and follow them. I went on sitting on the track where they had left me, and a great loneliness crept over me. Undoubtedly the *tarans* or the Shining Ones would get me and I would never see anyone I loved again. Tears poured out of my eyes and down my cheeks, and I leaned my head on my knees and sobbed out loud with tiredness and hopelessness. Then it happened.

"Wise Child!" said a voice. There was sympathy in it. I looked up, and there was Juniper, sitting on her donkey, looking down at me. She climbed down with a lithe, youthful movement and, before I knew what was happening, had bent down and wiped the tears from my cheeks with a handkerchief. I stopped crying, mainly out of surprise, I think, and she picked me up in her arms and swung me onto the saddle.

"Poor baby!" she said. My legs did not reach the stirrups, but she held me firmly onto the saddle and spoke gently to the donkey, which began to walk. It was all very surprising. It was surprising too to notice that the donkey's panniers were filled with blackberries, with a few large mushrooms lying on top of them—it had never occurred to me before that Juniper ate, as other people did.

Quite soon we came upon my cousins, waiting a couple of fields away to teach me a lesson. They were startled by the sight of the donkey and Juniper in the gathering darkness, and perhaps even more by the sight of me in the saddle. I did not know whether I felt smug or shy.

"She wouldn't walk," said Conor defensively, by way of explanation.

"Her legs are short," Juniper replied, without judgment.

The troop of children followed us, always the same distance behind, and I could hear them whispering and giggling. One of them—it was surely Seumas—called out, rudely and daringly, "Teach us a spell." I looked sideways at Juniper, but she just smiled to herself and said nothing. She was silent in a particular way of her own that made me feel as close to her as if we were having a conversation. She spoke only once again, which was as we approached the village and began to see the comforting rushlights peep out from people's homes.

"You may be too tired to walk today, but you'll be a great traveler one day," she said. "You're not Finbar's daughter for nothing." Then she lifted me off the donkey and set me down, and I stood rather foolishly in the road waiting for the others to catch up with me.

"WHAT DID the witch talk about?" Bride wanted to know.

"Nothing really," I said, keeping my secret.

"Just think!" Colman said admiringly. "You rode on Juniper's donkey."

"She's called Tillie," I said.

"It was only 'cause she's such a baby," said Mairi.

"Still, it was an adventure," said Morag.

IN THE NEXT several years I lost my baby plumpness and became thin and wiry. I was never an especially pretty child, and when I got the lice my grandmother, who could not see too well, hacked off my hair unevenly all over my head so that it stuck up here and there in spikes. The children laughed at me, but I did not mind very much—I was not interested in my appearance just then. When Colman wasn't in school, the two of us ran wild together like a pair of rabbits, both of us barefoot in summer. In winter, however, I wore neat leather shoes, while Colman wore an old patched pair of boots with flapping soles. His clothes were very worn and much too small for him. It did not occur to me to pity him, however. My main feeling toward him was one of envy because he went to school. I had gone for a little while to a school for girls run by an old woman in the village, but once she had taught us to read and write, something only a few of us mastered, there was nothing else to learn but spinning and sewing, both of which I loathed.

This meant, in the winter days at least, that I was obliged to spend a good deal of time at home, which I was sorry to do. Finbar, of course, had long since sailed away on his great voyage, which left only my grandmother as a companion. She, I seemed to remember, had once been quick on her feet, busy about the house, cleaning and cooking. Now she sat before the fire all day, dozing in her chair most of the time, too weary to spin or even to talk. Once she had been such a grand storyteller, such a singer—I had laughed, and wept, and been terrified by her stories, sometimes actually putting my hands over my ears because I could not bear any more.

"No. I don't want to know!" Then: "Tell me. Go on, tell me." There were no stories anymore, just that clouded, puzzled look in her eyes.

"Finbar?" she had said to me once, and I had said in a frightened voice, "You remember, Finbar went away. He'll be back soon."

Our eating got more and more haphazard. My grandmother never prepared anything now, and it never occurred to me to try to cook, any more than I tried to clean up the house. My aunt did her best to sort us out from time to time.

One summer day I went to see my cousins and said, "Granny's too tired to get up today." My aunt's tired, pretty face looked up from the washtub and she started drying her hands at once.

"I'll just go around to see," she said, and put on her shawl. Later on that day she told me.

"What will I do, then?" I said in a very loud, angry voice that hid how scared I was. Then I answered myself: "I know. I'll come and live with you and Colman."

My aunt slowly shook her head and lifted me onto her lap, something she did not often have time to do.

"Wise Child, you know we love you," she said, "but

there's no room. And there's not enough food for the children I've got already. And in any case, Uncle Gregor . . ."
Aunt Morag was mortally afraid of Uncle Gregor.

I knew that what she said was true. I had often seen the
children in bed, five of them crammed together, which I
would have hated, and in the same room as my uncle and
aunt. I suddenly remembered how when my grandmother,
in her good days, had baked a cake or made a stew, they had
devoured it desperately, and how once when I had taken the
last oatcake in my thoughtless way, Bride's eyes had filled
with tears. I was a proud child who loved my own bed, my
clean smock, my good leather shoes that Finbar had bought
me. And I liked to eat.

"So what will happen to me?" I began to wail. But I
knew the answer before she began to tell me.

IN OUR VILLAGE, which prided itself on taking care of those
who needed it, we had an institution called "the auction."
When a child's parents died, or sometimes if a woman was
left alone in the world, the village would gather together
after Mass, standing in a circle on the piece of grass in front
of the small stone church; the priest would preside, and
together they would all work out who needed the service of
the homeless one, or, more often, who could be persuaded
to put up with her or him.

"But what about Finbar?" I said desperately, trying to
think of a way out.

"It's like him to be away when he's needed," my aunt
said. "The Lord knows when he'll be back. Where could
you live, chick, in the meantime? Who will look after you?"
I longed to say, "I will look after myself," but I knew that

I could not do it. When my hair was still long I could not wash it or plait it myself. I could not make a soup or a stew, nor bake a cake or a loaf, though hunger had taught me how to make porridge. I wept again, for my helplessness, for the public humiliation of the auction.

"It's not so bad," my aunt comforted me. "There are good women in this village, and if they are not good to you, they will have me to reckon with."

It was not that that I minded so much, though. It was more that I had thought myself special, a child to be prized, and now all of a sudden I was a thing like a pot or pan, to be bargained over.

So I sat and wept throughout Mass, and afterward the priest led me out to the waiting ring of villagers outside. He was an Irishman, with the crinkly red hair and the flushing skin that was different from the blond hair, the blue eyes, and the clear pallor of most of our people. His hand rested heavily on my shoulder. I wriggled to get out from underneath it, but he tightened his hold.

"In the name of Our Lord Jesus Christ, who bade us to care for the homeless and the fatherless, I am asking you this morning to find a home for this little sister of ours, reminding you that charity is the essence of our faith, and that you will be piling up a reward for yourselves in heaven."

Despite this incentive there was a long silence. I hung my head. Nobody wanted me, it seemed. Then Brigid from the Beyond spoke.

"We could do with a girl's pair of hands about the place, especially just now with the harvest coming on, but she's really too small, and she's never worked. We always said she was a spoiled one."

Greta the Scarred spoke next.

"I could train her to work," she said. "There are no lazy girls in my house." I had seen her children, anxious and worn, little workhorses before they were eight years old. They did not get to school much, and when they did they had swollen eyes from weeping and the marks of beating on them. I could feel my aunt tense beside me.

"What other offers?" said the priest, apparently indifferent as to who should take me in. There was another long silence, and I began pressing my nails tightly into my palms to resist the fate of being taken by Greta.

"I will be glad to care for her, if she would like that," Juniper's deep, husky voice suddenly said. I had not noticed her before, but there she was, a head taller than anyone else, standing in the circle directly facing the priest. They made a contrast—the fair-skinned, blushing priest and the dark, glowing woman. Fillan's hand tightened even harder on my shoulder—there was no love lost between him and Juniper.

"She shall have a Christian home," he said dismissively.

"I will send her to Mass, of course," said Juniper. Fillan ignored her, but I could feel his hesitation. A murmur was running around the circle. Nobody liked Greta very much, and they did not want to entrust a child to her. Perhaps too they were afraid of making Juniper angry, since they feared her powers. In any case they felt a pull toward Juniper—she was their magic woman exactly as Fillan was their priest. They did not care to have to choose between them.

"Why not let Wise Child herself choose?" said Juniper. The people murmured again. I had turned scarlet with the embarrassment of this terrible occasion and the agony of having to choose. For the first time in my life I looked squarely at Juniper. I saw her slender height, the laughter lines in her face—even at this moment she had a merry expression, her lips parted over strong white teeth. She had deep, dark eyes that had looked on sorrow somewhere; she wore a dark-red dress (our women dressed themselves in brown or black) and a great ruby on her finger. Under the big straw hat her skin was a rich olive and her hair glossy black, like my own.

I glanced at Greta, at her small, bitter face closed like a trap, at the long, scrawny arms with which she slapped her children. I looked too at the two children standing beside her, with their cunning, suspicious faces. I could not possibly live with Greta; yet Juniper, we all knew, worked for the Devil, and if I worked for her I might be damned forever. I wrung my hands at my terrible predicament.

Just then Aunt Morag, poor, fearful Aunt Morag, who lived in dread of Gregor's temper and who rarely raised her voice outside her own home, spoke up in a loud, clear voice.

"There is Finbar's opinion to be considered," she said.

"Finbar?" said Fillan in surprise.

"Before he went away, he foresaw the possibility of his mother's death, and that Wise Child would need a home until he returned. He said that if that should happen, she was to go to Juniper, that he had asked Juniper to undertake this for him, and that she had agreed."

Juniper neither confirmed nor denied this; she just smiled. It took me a few moments to understand it. Child as I was, I knew perfectly well that Aunt Morag was lying. It would not occur to Finbar to plan for my future in that way—he would never have anticipated the problem—so Aunt Morag must be lying for a purpose. The purpose, I knew at once, was to give me a sort of cue, the cue that it was all right to live with Juniper, no matter what I had been told about her. I responded instantly and automatically.

"I want to live with Juniper," I said.

The priest blushed more furiously than ever.

"Is there not a Christian home that will take this child?" he asked. The people murmured amongst themselves again. They knew very well that Juniper could afford to feed me better than any of them could. It was all very well for Fillan—no hungry children waited in his house.

Uncle Gregor, perhaps not wanting to be outdone by Aunt Morag, perhaps feeling that it was time to exert some sort of patriarchal right over his female possessions, intervened at this point.

"If it was Finbar's wish . . ." he said. (Perhaps I do him an injustice. Perhaps he too was genuinely anxious about what would become of me.) Fillan knew that he was defeated—the anger showed clearly enough in his face.

"Very well then," he said, "the *cailleach* shall take her." There was a slight shock of surprise at hearing him use this word. It was a word you used behind people's backs, not to their faces.

"Good," said Juniper. "Wise Child, you will need to sit with your grandmother before her funeral. After the funeral Tillie and I will come and collect you." She gave me her warm friendly smile, slipped through the crowd, and was gone. The crowd began to disperse, too, not in its usual gossipy fashion, but quickly and silently, as if something distasteful had been completed, and then I was walking home with my aunt and cousins. I walked apart, angry at my public ordeal, but above all frightened. What had come to me that I, alone of everyone I knew, had to live with a witch? Nobody spoke about it, but about halfway home Colman slipped his hand into mine. I did not acknowledge that he had touched me, but I did not let go.

It was the custom to sit up with our dead, and that night my aunt and I dutifully took our seats beside the body of the old woman, who now looked so different that I did not feel she was my granny at all. They had tidied her hair and dressed her in a gray dress that I recognized, but it was the expression on her face that was quite different. After what seemed an age, Colman slipped into the room and began to sit too. It was indescribably boring just sitting there, and I wept quite a lot—not for my grandmother, who seemed to be all right, but for myself, who was henceforward a lost soul. My aunt heated some soup on the fire at about midnight, which was a great treat—I realized that I was starving—but soon after that I seemed unable to keep my eyes open any longer. The next thing I remember is seeing bright sunlight shining on the bed, and Colman and I were both lying in it together. Colman was still asleep, and so was my aunt, still propped awkwardly in her chair. I thought, *I want my grandmother buried so that life can begin again,* but then I remembered what that life was to be. I wept quietly. Colman woke up and saw the tears on my cheeks. He was never a child of many words.

"Finbar may be back anytime," he said.

"I'm frightened," I sobbed.

Colman did not try to comfort me, knowing that in my situation he would be equally frightened himself. Later in the day my other cousins, less kind than he, remembered all the child gossip they had ever heard about Juniper. Like me they were fascinated and excited by the idea of magic but also afraid of it, partly because they thought it was wicked and also because they were afraid it might hurt them. It was said that witches brought diseases, poisoned crops and animals, and killed people they did not like.

"She has these two huge cats that are her familiars, and they talk with her just like people!"

"She rides on her broom. On moonlit nights you can see her outline against the moon."

"She meets with the other witches sometimes, and they all dance without their clothes on, and they . . ." Mairi went off into a gust of giggles and began to whisper something in Seumas's ear so that he began to giggle too.

"They say that under her house there are enormous caves with big piles of jewels—rubies and emeralds, gold and pearls."

"She gives you honey drinks that make things look all different."

"I bet the Evil One"—Domnall crossed himself—"comes there often . . . that there are ghosts in her house . . . unquiet spirits . . . that she summons up the dead . . . that there are murdered children there."

I stamped my foot.

"Stop it!" I said. "Finbar will be home soon, and then I will go to live with him." But I was very scared.

My face was washed, my poor uneven hair was combed back and stuck down with grease, which Juniper told me later made my eyes look enormous and my forehead white and bare. I was put into a black gown, too big for me, that I kept tripping over, and I wore my good leather shoes that I was so proud of.

My uncle, Conor, and some other men carried my grandmother's coffin out of the house, and I was glad to see it go, for in the hot weather the body seemed to make a strange, sweetish smell in the house that I hated, and I was bored with all the sitting still, and the watching. Watching what? There was nothing to see.

I had chosen the things I was going to take with me— a winter smock and a summer one, my smart stockings my grandmother had knitted in wheel stitch, my hood and cloak, a doll called Nan, a rope for skipping, and a mouse Colman had once carved for me in wood. My aunt packed them in my basket with an apple and kissed me tenderly.

"You know that we love you, Wise Child, and that you are our kin. If you are in trouble, Gregor and I will help you. You are like our own child." *Not enough like your child to live with you,* I thought angrily, but I was sobbing too much to speak.

So I walked behind my grandmother's coffin with my eyes swollen with crying, my throat dry and full of a lump I did not seem able to swallow, wearing the ugly black dress that was too big for me. On the way to the church it started to rain, and before we got there we were soaked, hair like rats' tails, shoes squelching along the track, which was dissolving into mud. The rain matched my mood, the sadness that lay on me like a weight, the sadness that my grandmother was shut away in a box and would soon be shut in the earth, the sadness that I was lost and unloved and had a terrible fate before me. From deep in my memory came the recollection of another loss, of realizing, not swiftly but slowly, that Maeve the Fair was lost to me forever. I was now nine years old and nobody wanted me except a witch.

"I bet she'll make you her apprentice," Seumas said. "Witches choose little girls to be their apprentices. Then you'll be a witch too."

"Shut up!" Bride said. Obviously Aunt Morag had rebuked the children for frightening me.

"The first thing I will do when I'm a witch," I said to Seumas, "is turn you into something horrible—a tadpole." Already I had a picture of myself stirring some fetid brew over a fire with bits of live creatures chopped up in it. My heart turned over with fright and disgust.

Juniper was not in the church, but when the coffin was carried out into the churchyard, she was in the group that stood around the grave. She stood respectfully, with a thoughtful look on her face, as Fillan Priest said the prayers, and when the coffin was lowered and people threw flowers down onto the lid, Juniper threw some poppies and cornflowers she had been carrying. Tillie was tethered by the churchyard gate, and when the funeral was over, Juniper stood waiting for me there. No good-byes were said—I was still a part of the village—but people waited and watched while Juniper picked up my bag and tied it onto Tillie's back. The two of us set off together in silence, one on each side of the donkey. I looked back only once, when we were a long way down the road. They had all gone by then, except for Colman, who was wearing a white woolen smock, much patched at the elbows. (My aunt could not afford to dress us all in black for her mother's funeral.) He stood there, a tiny white speck in the road, still waving to me. I waved back. As we turned the last corner and disappeared, he gave the cry of the curlew that we had so often used to summon each other, stealing secretly out of bed on summer nights. I wept for the life that was gone.

2

The White House

I T WAS a long way to Juniper's house. We passed along the side of a field full of ripe barley, and across another field, and through a gate, and over a stream by a plank bridge. Later that bridge was to terrify me, but I was too frightened of Juniper at that moment to have fear to spare for the narrow plank and the rushing water. I was sniffing back the tears. Juniper did not mention my tears, but I did not feel she ignored them either. She just walked along, occasionally speaking to Tillie and sometimes humming a little tune to herself.

It was raining again, and I could feel the wet squidging horribly in my shoes; miserably I knew that the brown leather would stain my lovely stockings, and I wept again because of that. I walked more and more slowly, but this time Juniper did not suggest that I ride on Tillie's back. The track had started to wind very steeply uphill. It seemed unfair that I had to puff and pant as well as cry. The two of us labored up the track—Juniper had stopped humming now—toward the white house with the stone walls. I had always lived in a little round house made of timber and mud—nearly everyone I knew except Juniper lived in that sort of house.

"Stop a minute," said Juniper. "It's misty today, but it's a wonderful view." There was the village with all its little beehive-shaped houses and gardens, and the barns and fields in different colors, and the Big Ditch beyond that and the palisades that were built to keep away the foreign devils, and then farther away the blue heath and the shore and the sea, and the distant islands, and beyond that the mountains whose peaks were in sunlight. It was a glorious sight. In the village itself there were tiny antlike figures of people.

"Nearly home," said Juniper.

We reached the lip of the cliff and passed over it. We were on the roof of the world now. The white house was very close, bigger even than I remembered it. We passed through a gate, through a wilderness of flowers—nobody grew *flowers*, just things to eat. Then we went up some shallow steps and in at the door. My heart was beating very fast, so it was quite hard to breathe.

My first feeling was one of space—it was the biggest room I had ever seen, with a flight of stairs leaving it from one corner. In the middle was the great hearth, and although it was August there was already a fire burning there that filled the house with the comforting smell of peat. Around the fireplace was a kind of step with cushions upon it, and there were two huge cats already sitting there just as the children had said there would be. Seeing me look at them, Juniper introduced them.

"This is Pearl," she said, waving her hand at the white

cat. "And this is Ruby"—indicating the gray one. Both cats looked up as if they were curious about me and then stared straight in front of them again.

"Why Ruby?" I asked, speaking for the first time since leaving the village. "She's not red."

"It's her eyes," said Juniper. "They glow in the dark like rubies. Besides, I love rubies."

In front of the fireplace was a carved chair where I knew Juniper must sit, and beside it was a small chair with a green cushion.

"That is for you," said Juniper.

"For me?"

"I was expecting you."

I sat down in the chair, and Juniper started unfastening my wet shoes and easing off my stockings.

"How fine your stockings are!" she said admiringly. In the village we never praised another's possessions, still less their children or their animals, for fear of attracting the Evil Eye. Her praise did seem odd.

Then she helped me pull off the clammy dress that I hated and wrapped a soft blanket around me. I sat in my green chair, which was very comfortable, and Juniper brought me a hot drink. I remembered about the honey drink that made you see everything differently.

"What's in it?" I asked suspiciously, thinking, *I'll have to eat and drink* sometime.

"It's tea," said Juniper. "One I drink on special occasions, made out of my very best herbs."

I sipped it carefully, waiting for it to make me feel funny and ill, but it tasted so delicious, and I had been feeling so cold, that I could not stop drinking it. It was sweet without

* * *

I TURNED to the staircase. It was very remarkable. At the bottom of the stairs, and halfway up, and again at the top, the carpenter had used the stair posts to carve flowers—poppies and pinks and roses and convolvulus—and along the banisters he had carved animals—gentle deer, and lambs and dogs and lions. I thought it was the most interesting staircase I had ever seen, though I had not seen many. Beside the staircase an enormous window of greeny leaded glass looked sideways over the village and past it to the sea, and the window was curtained in a silky fabric of forest green with touches of red and blue gleaming in it like metal, and once again the motif of poppies and roses and pinks and convolvulus was repeated. I touched the curtains with reverence—they were so beautiful. There was a thick carpet on the stairs, and it led my feet up to another floor with doors opening off it. The doors were closed, and it was frightening to open them.

However, my curiosity was too great for me to resist, and I discovered that there were two big bedrooms, each with a carved bed and a white cover on the bed. Each had big dark cabinets. Remembering what Seumas had said, I shuddered. One of the rooms had another tiny room opening off it, almost like a cupboard, just big enough to hold a small bed, with a pretty rag rug beside it. It was a cozy little place, a nest with the walls painted in orange flowers.

Another small staircase led upward from this floor. I climbed up a few steps, knowing that this must lead to the attic. I could see the small white door at the top, with a beautiful ivory handle. I was so sure that this door must be locked that I could not resist trying it, but to my surprise it opened half an inch. My heart began to beat very fast as I decided to explore further, but just then I heard Juniper's step downstairs. I shut the door quickly, and ran softly down the wooden staircase and back down the carpeted one.

Juniper smiled at me. "Do you like my house?" she wanted to know.

"It's pretty," I said coldly.

"Hungry?" she asked. I was hungry, but I was fearful, too. Suppose she put magic in the food? It was a terrible dilemma. I decided to let her know that I suspected her.

"Seumas said you might make spells in the food," I mumbled. I blushed as soon as I had said it and looked away from her. There was a moment's silence, and suddenly I was terror-stricken. Now the kindly mask would fall off and I would see the witch as she really was—wicked and cruel and out to get me in her power.

But to my amazement she laughed, a big, gurgling laugh that was irresistibly jolly.

"Why don't you come and help me prepare supper, and then you can see whether I put any spells on it. Then . . . if we both eat the same things . . . will that make you feel safer?"

I nodded again, embarrassed now, and went with her into the dairy to cut the peppered cheese and to pour the foaming yellow milk. We supped off that and big slices of dark bread, and there was wallflower-dark honey, and some sweet blueberry mess that I liked particularly. Juniper was meticulous about dividing every dish, or slice, in half, which annoyed me rather since I had begun to feel silly about my fears. But I was terribly hungry—I had eaten very little in the previous twenty-four hours and for the last months of my grandmother's life had survived mostly on oatcakes and porridge. Nature was too much for me. I simply gave up worrying about spells and so enjoyed my meal very much.

"I KNOW A SPELL," I told Juniper when my hunger was somewhat appeased. I didn't want her to think she was the only one who knew magic. "Well, it's more of a charm, really. For the toothache. Niall taught it me."

"That boy with the sad eyes who lives in the house opposite the church?" (I was to be astonished at how carefully Juniper had observed us all.)

"I'll tell you if you like." I could never resist any chance to recite, so I plunged at once into the charm.

> *"Peter sat weeping on a marble stone.*
> *Jesus came and said,*
> *'What aileth thee, Peter?'*
> *He answereth and said,*
> *'My Lord and my God.'*
> *He that can say this, and believeth it for My Sake,*
> *Never no more shall have the toothache."*

I finished this with a fine dramatic flourish.

"Well!" said Juniper. "Does it work?"

"I'm not sure," I said truthfully. "I only half had toothache once, and I had a feeling it was about to get better anyway."

"Toothache *is* a difficult one," Juniper admitted, as one magician to another. "I expect I'd have some other ideas if

I racked my brains. Chamomile might help a bit. Now I must go and shut up the chickens—there's a wicked old fox on the prowl—and perhaps you could wash the plates?"

I did not want to admit that I was the only girl in those parts who had never washed plates—that I had always left it all to my grandmother—so although I hated doing those sorts of jobs, I lifted the big water jug that stood in a sink near the table and poured some water into a bowl. I used a sort of scratchy twig thing to take the stickiness off the plates. Luckily they were not very dirty. Then I found the cloth and dried them, and although a *little* of the stickiness came off on the cloth and made it dirty, I more or less got it done.

Juniper meanwhile had come back bearing an armful of driftwood, and quite soon the salty flames began twisting green and blue around the wood. It was lovely to watch.

"Would you like me to tell you a story?" Juniper asked. "I'm a good storyteller."

I said nothing, feeling that the distance between us had become much too narrow over supper. I had even told her what I knew about the stars—how my father used to take me out at night and hold me on his shoulder to teach me the names of the planets. And how in the summer sometimes we would lie out at night on the hill with a blanket or two and watch the great constellations wheel about us. I would fall asleep and wake up and find that Orion, my favorite, had moved toward the horizon and that other stars were looking down on me. Suddenly I wanted Finbar very badly. As if Juniper could read my mind, she said, very quietly, "He will be back, Wise Child. In a while. Meanwhile, you will have to make do with me."

Without further speech she picked up the lute, tuned it, and began to sing me a song about three knights. One wore red, one wore green, and one wore yellow. (The chorus went "Oh, the red, the green, and the yellow." There was also a bit that went "The harp, the lute, the pipe, the flute, the cymbal, Sweet is the treble violin." It all made such an impression on me that I still catch myself singing it from time to time, although Juniper never sang it again after that night.) All three of the knights went on a quest, but only the yellow knight was lucky and won the lady, probably because he was the nicest of them all.

I liked it very much. Then Juniper told me a story about a juggler who got cleverer and cleverer and cleverer and learned to juggle with more and more and more balls, and got more and more and more conceited with each ball he took on, until one day he juggled in front of the emperor and dropped the whole lot. It was really very funny, seeing how conceited the juggler was from looking at the proud expression on Juniper's face, and then how crestfallen he was after the catastrophe, but she went on to explain how the kitchenmaid who had always loved him, and whom he had thought beneath him, came and comforted him; for the first time he truly appreciated her and realized he loved her.

"I can teach you how to juggle if you like," Juniper said. "Not as many balls as the juggler in the story. Three or four, perhaps." She had some wormy apples in a basket— windfalls that had come down before the crop was ripe— and she showed me what to do.

"The trick," she said, "is getting the rhythm right. Da-da, da-da, da-da, like that. You throw the apple up with your left hand, and just as it is coming to the top of its flight, you throw the next apple from right to left."

Even with this advice I couldn't do it, and I kept dropping the apples and giggling and trying again. Juniper wasn't very good at it, either, though she was better than I was. I forgot all about her being a witch and was laughing and bouncing apples off the furniture, until suddenly one fell on the cards. Immediately Juniper stopped laughing and became very serious indeed.

"You've changed the cards," she said. I knew that she was going to be angry with me now, and I hung my head.

"I'm sorry. They were there, and I played with them," I said. I think I would have lied if I had thought I could get away with it.

"Oh, *that* doesn't matter," Juniper said. "It is just *what* you have done with the cards that I am interested in."

"I was just playing around," I said wretchedly.

"Playing around *is* what people do with those cards. Then you look at the pattern and see what it tells you."

"It doesn't tell me anything," I said, looking doubtfully at the jumble of cards.

"It tells me something, though."

"What?"

"That this is the right place for you. I thought it was."

IT WAS GROWING dark now, and Juniper took a long taper from the shelf over the hearth, touched it to the fire, and lit a small candlestick also standing on the shelf. As she straightened herself from this task and handed me the candle, she suddenly looked strange in the firelight, unnaturally tall and a little fierce. At the same time I was aware of the darkness waiting for me at the top of the stairs. I turned away from her, ashamed to tell her that a big girl like me was frightened of the dark and still more frightened of whatever it was she might have hidden in her dark cabinets. I wanted Aunt Morag and the children and the village, and all the things and people that I was used to. My feet moved very slowly up the staircase, and the shadow of the candle danced mockingly on the wall. My hand slid around the doorknob of the big room on the right, and I slipped through the door, feeling very tiny in the vastness of the room. I put the candle down beside the bed, took off my smock, and dropped it on the floor. I thought I had better not walk too close to the bed lest a hand should come out and grab my ankle, so I took a running jump at the bed, which gave a little squeal as I landed on it. I pulled the blankets and sheets close.

If I had not been so scared, I would have admired the fineness of the sheets, but my attention was on the way the candlelight flickered over the walls and up into the high, high ceiling. Over one cabinet was a big, dark hole, and straining my eyes to see into the shadow, I could see a face with a blunt nose and a big chin looking out of it. Perhaps if I blew out my candle, it would think that I had gone away—I knew that magic creatures were easily deceived. I half sat up and blew out the candle and then with a little moan lay back and pulled the sheets and blankets over my head.

Now, however, the darkness seemed sort of creaky, and I thought I could hear breathing. When I put my head on the pillow, I could hear a steady *thump, thump, thump,* and I imagined a monster walking up and down the passage out-

side my door. He had a body like a man but a head like a
pig. It was worse with the candle out than it had been when
it was alight. The darkness felt heavy and stuffy, as if it was
pressing the breath out of me. I began to cry, with tiny
quiet sobs at first, then with big noisy ones.

Just then the door opened and Juniper came in carrying
a lamp, which she held up high.

"Why, Wise Child!" she said. She came and sat down on
the bed, and suddenly the room seemed much more cheerful
as she filled it with her warm presence. "What is it?"

I thought of all the things that had scared me.

"I'm frightened," I wailed.

"What of?" asked Juniper, who, I was later to discover,
always liked to know the details of things.

Without stopping to think, as if I was talking to some
other person altogether, I told Juniper, between sobs, how
my cousins had said that her cabinets were full of ghosts, or
bodies, and about how she flew on her broomstick, and
about the jewel cave, and about the honey drink that made
you see everything differently. I heaved a great sobbing sigh
when I got to the end, and I felt a lot better. She had
listened carefully to all of it.

"That would be enough to frighten anyone," she said
warmly. "I think you've been very brave with all that to
worry about. As for the cabinets, they are full of very
boring things, you know—we'll look at them by daylight
and you can see for yourself. For the rest . . . there are
things about the way I live that are different from the life
you are used to, but I think you will rather like it when
you get used to it."

"You mean there isn't any magic, or spells, or anything

of that sort?" I said, immediately disappointed now that my fear had subsided.

"I didn't say that. It's just that magic gets quite ordinary when you live with it, you know. You'll soon see."

There was silence between us for a little, and then she said, "You know, this room is much too big for you, Wise Child. You will rattle around in it like a hailstone on a roof. In my bedroom there is a tiny room with a little bed in it, just the right size for you, and now that you know that there is no need to be frightened of me, it will be just right for you. Would you like to sleep in there?"

I nodded. It sounded lovely. Juniper wrapped a quilt around me, lifted me up in her arms as she had done those years before on the road, and carried me out of the frightening room, across the passage, and to the little bed in the tiny room with the orange flowers. She tucked the bedclothes in around me. Suddenly I felt wonderfully warm and cozy, and terribly sleepy. Whatever the horrors of the house, they seemed to have nothing to do with me now. Later I half-woke to hear Juniper quietly breathing in her part of the room (she wasn't out on her broomstick, then?) and that made me feel glad and safe. When I next woke up, the sunshine was brilliant on the orange flowers, the sky was blue, and I could hear birds singing. I jumped out of bed onto the bright rag rug, pulled on my brown smock—there was no sign of the black dress and I was not sorry—and ran barefoot down the stairs, curious to see what Juniper would do or say today.

3

The Herb Garden

DO YOU REALLY have a broomstick?" I asked Juniper. "Of course. Over there behind the door. How else would I sweep the floor?"

This morning the big room was quiet and peaceful. Juniper was busy putting wood into her bread oven—three loaves had already been set to rise on the table. She was singing as she worked; seeing her flushed and busy, and the house so pleasant and normal, it was hard to believe that only last night I had felt myself in danger. The sun shone upon the scrubbed table. The fire had gone out, leaving a pile of ashes on the hearth; Ruby and Pearl were nowhere to be seen.

Before coming downstairs, I had looked at myself in Juniper's big bronze mirror decorated with scrolls and tendrils, and as if looking at myself once had created the habit, my eyes now went automatically to the round mirror over the fireplace. When I looked in this mirror, however, I did not see my pale face, swollen eyelids, and spiky hair re-

flected. Instead I could see the village street, quite clearly,
with old Donal limping in his bandy way down the middle
of it, two of the women talking at a doorstep, and another
sweeping out her house. I exclaimed with astonishment.

Juniper, who was pouring creamy yellow milk out of a
big jug, looked up with interest.

"What can you see?" she asked curiously.

"Donal and Margaret," I said shortly. The sight of the
milk had made me aware that I was, once again, extremely
hungry. It was wonderful that there was plenty of oatmeal
and bread and honey. Soon my stomach felt round and full.

"Why does that mirror show the village?" I asked Juniper.

"It's a magic mirror," she said matter-of-factly. "After
breakfast," she went on, "you must have a look at Daisy and
the rest of the garden. Then we'd better do some lessons."

"In magic?" I asked. I was both curious and scared.

Juniper laughed.

"I thought we'd begin with reading, writing, astronomy,
fairy stories—that kind of thing. Later on we'll do a bit of
Latin."

"Girls don't learn Latin," I told her. "It unfits them for
marriage." (I was quoting my Uncle Gregor's views on the
education of girls.) "And I never heard of a school that
taught fairy tales."

"All learned people learn Latin," she said. "It's bound to
come in useful. Fairy tales, on the other hand, are about real
life."

I could not make head or tail of this, so I changed the
subject slightly.

"Will you beat me?" I asked with interest.

"What do you think?"

"I think you will. All teachers beat children to make them behave."

"Will you be disappointed if I don't?"

I thought this over. It was a difficult point.

"I don't like anything that *hurts*," I said finally. "On the other hand I don't want to be a spoiled child. More than I am already, that is."

"*Are* you spoiled, Wise Child?"

"My cousins always said so. And Brigid from the Beyond, if you noticed at the . . . after Mass the other day . . ."

"It's not how I see you. At all."

AFTER BREAKFAST Juniper began to wash up the dishes, and she asked me to sweep the floor. I fetched the broomstick to humor her, but I thought I'd better have the housework problem out with her right away.

"I don't like cleaning or dusting or cooking or doing dishes, or any of those things," I explained to her. "And I don't usually do it. I find it boring, you see."

"Everyone has to do those things," she said.

"Rich people don't," I pointed out.

Juniper laughed, as she often did at things I said in those early days, but at once became quite serious.

"They miss a lot of fun," she said. "But quite apart from that—keeping yourself clean, preparing the food you are going to eat, clearing it away afterward—that's what life's *about*, Wise Child. When people forget that, or lose touch with it, then they lose touch with other important things as well."

"Men don't do those things."

"Exactly. Also, as you clean the house up, it gives you time to tidy yourself up inside—you'll see."

I was surprised to find that I quite liked sweeping the floor. Partly it was that I wanted to get a good look at the broomstick. I folded the two smaller carpets and laid them on the flight of steps outside the front door, and then, since Juniper had disappeared into the dairy, I took a careful look at the broom. It had a straight gray branch for a handle and a bundle of twigs, exactly like my grandmother's broom. There wasn't much dust around, but I swept what there was down the cracks between the flags and put all the carpets carefully back into place. Then I started dusting, though there were so many interesting things to clean that I did not seem to make very much progress. Apart from the lute and the harp, which I could not resist twanging, and the cards, which I kept well away from, there was a sort of stone, purple with a network of crystals at its heart. There was a big bowl of sweet-smelling herbs that gave the room a lovely scent I had noted the night before. There were tiny vases made out of silver, crystal, and what looked like pearl; there was a huge piece of jet; there was a tube with a tiny hole in the top of it, and when you looked through it you saw a pattern in bright colors that spread and changed.

Juniper seemed gratifyingly pleased with my labors when she returned.

"You see? You do it beautifully," she said. I preened myself.

We passed out of the back door into a little red-tiled courtyard, with Tillie's stable on one side and beyond it a big room which Juniper used for drying herbs. Some branches of the plant we call queen's feather were spread out thinly on the floor, giving the room a scent like new-mown hay. On the other side of the yard was a small barn that housed a dozen hens, a lot of hay, and Daisy, a small red-and-white cow. Only later, when Juniper taught me to milk her, did I discover that Daisy could be cross and obstinate, just like a person, shoving you just when you least expected it or kicking the pail over.

Beyond the courtyard was the herb garden, separated from the meadow by a hedge, and now suddenly I understood the plan of Juniper's garden. She had about a hide of land, and it made a circle or wheel with her house at the center. The herbs were in neat sections of the wheel, fenced in by little hedges of their own. In the inner sections of the wheel were the smaller herbs and the ones Juniper used most often—eyebright, pennyroyal, primrose, violet, chamomile, heartsease, and marjoram (brought back from distant travels, like a number of Juniper's plants). Then there were bigger plants—lovage, feverfew, woodruff, tansy, borage, iris, lily, foxglove, marigold, comfrey, vervain, hyssop, rosemary and wormwood, lavender and southernwood. (I did not know the names of most of these plants at the time and I may be making up some of them, but these were the sorts of plants we usually worked with.) Beyond these, on the outer rim of the wheel, were some ragged plants that the eye passed over quickly—nightshade, henbane, thorn apple, white poppy, mandrake. They were dusty and unappealing.

"Better leave them alone," said Juniper. "They can make you dreadfully ill."

"Why have them then?" I asked curiously.

"They have their uses. Everything has its time and place."

* * *

THE HERB GARDEN was quite unlike the flower garden at the front of the house, where plants grew, thickly planted, in beautiful wildness. The herbs were neat, businesslike, pretty in their own way; but it was clear that Juniper grew them for quite another purpose. At that first glimpse I had no idea what a labor those herbs would come to be to me—the hours I would spend cutting, removing seeds, shredding roots, turning and drying, crushing seeds in a mortar, steeping, boiling, infusing, bruising, distilling—making ointments and essences, tinctures and teas. How I was to sweat and ache, weep and grumble, over them!

As it was, I gave them a brief glance before we went inside to start lessons.

First Juniper had me read to her, and I could see she was impressed.

"You're a wonderful reader, Wise Child," she said. Then she handed me a wax tablet in a bone frame, and I wrote slanty writing on it with a silver stylus. I wrote my name and the names of some saints. It was not very good, but Juniper said, "The stylus is a present. To remember your first day as a scholar." Then we did sums, which I liked. After that she taught me a little English.

"*English,*" I said, scornful, like all my countrymen, of our neighbors.

"You never know when it will come in useful," she said. I could see that my education was going to be an unusual one.

"Better than spinning and weaving," I remarked.

"Oh, you'll learn those, too."

I groaned. "That's what girls do. I hate doing what girls do."

"Here you will never learn anything just because girls do it. But it's a pity not to do things just because girls do them. Work must be done for its own sake."

She paused. "What is difficult about learning—any kind of learning—is that you have to give up what you know already to make room for the new ideas. Until you get used to it, it makes you feel very silly. But then the reward is that you can suddenly do new things. Children are much better at it than grownups. Especially if nobody beats them."

"I don't understand," I said crossly.

SHE ENDED by teaching me a long poem all about storms and clouds and rainbows and the moon—she made me repeat it after her while she got on with preparing our lunch.

After lunch, when I was feeling comfortably full again—*full*—*twice* in one day, too—and a bit drowsy, we went back to the herb garden, and at Juniper's suggestion I started collecting the seeds of the black mustard in a basket, while Juniper began picking leaves from the wormwood.

"Early afternoon is a good time to collect herbs," Juniper explained. "The dew has long since dried off them." As I collected the awl-shaped seeds, Juniper began to tell me about the sorts of plants you use to make sick people well.

Of course, everyone knows some things about making sick people well. They know that you rub goose grease on your chest to prevent a cough in the winter, that eel skins are good for rheumatism, that roast mouse sends away whooping cough, that if you shake hands with Mucky Peg it makes your warts go, that the water in which the blacksmith dips the red-hot horseshoe cures all sorts of things, especially measles—that sort of thing. And what mattered in all of these cures was saying the right words as you took the stuff. If you didn't get the words exactly right—and you often didn't—then you were stuck with your complaint. My people were great ones for reciting little rhymes whenever they did anything—when they were putting their clothes on, going on a journey, "smooring" the fire before they retired, or whatever it was.

Juniper's ideas were not like that at all. What the plant looked like, she said—whether it resembled the color of the disease, or had been the tree that sheltered Mary or on which Judas had hung himself—did not come into it. Nor did the words you said over the mixture. Two kinds of things made you better, according to Juniper. One was when something good was going on in your mind. The other was the juices and oils of some of the plants. Through chopping or shredding or crushing or steeping bits of the herbs, usually in the pure water of Juniper's well, you made a mixture, always the same sort of mixture from the same sort of plants, that made some bit of you feel better. It could be your eyes or your stomach, your skin or your bladder— any part of you, really.

"It's just a matter of learning what plants, or what mixtures of plants, encourage people to feel well."

"Don't they want to feel well?" I asked in surprise.

"Not always. Sometimes life is too difficult to be lived. So it's better to be sick for a bit."

"So what happens then?"

"You have to tease out the pain—in their minds, that is—like teasing burrs out of wool."

There were other things you did about pain, she explained to me. Willow bark, if you boiled it, was very good for painful rheumatics and fever. Then there were other plants that made people go to sleep until their bodies had begun to get better.

"One day I'll teach you all those things, Wise Child. When you're bigger."

In the middle of this explanation we moved indoors, and I began pounding the seeds until my arms ached and the sweat was running into my eyes.

"I don't like doing this much," I told Juniper. "I think plants are boring, anyway."

"Hard luck, Wise Child," she replied, but quite soon she suggested that it was time to stop for the day. We took cushions and sat out on the front steps. It was wonderful out there in the afternoon sun, and you could see for miles. The steps were so wide across that I could lie full length on them, and so broad that they comfortably supported my whole body. It was lovely to be held in their warmth. I could hear Juniper humming quietly to herself as she sat beside me—she sat stiller than anyone I had ever known—and then I drifted to sleep and dreamed of a boat far away from the island with a man at the tiller whose face I could not see. Yet I knew it was Finbar, my father.

Juniper's sudden exclamation woke me, and there, coming nervously through the yew hedge down below, looking very small at the bottom of the steps, was Colman.

As, wearily and doggedly, he began to climb the steps, he spotted me at the top of the flight and a brief smile passed over his face. When he drew nearer, I could see that he had tumbled over on his journey and that both his knees

were cut and bleeding. His bare feet too were cut and
scratched, his face and his smock were covered with white
dust, and there were two telltale runnels in the dust on his
cheeks. For a moment I felt shy at seeing him there, and
then all at once I was delighted and flew down the steps and
put my arms around him. Juniper had stood up, and she
looked down at us with a friendly smile.

"This is *Colman*," I said, shouting as I often did when I
was excited.

"I know," said Juniper. "That was a weary climb. Sit
down and rest and talk to Wise Child, and I'll bring you a
drink and some water to wash with."

Colman and I sat and looked at each other, he smiling a
tired, uncertain smile, I grinning broadly.

"Are you all right?" he whispered so that Juniper could
not hear. I nodded.

Juniper came back with a bowl of milk, which Colman
drank greedily. Then she brought out a basin of water and
a cloth, dipped the cloth in the water, and, squeezing it
out, handed it to Colman so that he could wash his hands
and face. Meanwhile, crouching on the steps, she gently
bathed his poor knees and feet.

"I'm going to learn Latin," I told Colman proudly while
this was going on.

"Girls don't . . . ouch . . . it unfits them for . . . ooh."

"It *is* sore, isn't it?" said Juniper sympathetically.

"All learned people learn Latin. She's going to teach me
about herbs, too, though that's pretty boring." Juniper
giggled but said nothing.

"We haven't done any magic yet," I went on.

When Juniper had finished washing Colman's feet, she

took a handful of leaves and pressed them gently on the cuts. "I'd sit like that for a bit, if I were you," she said, and went off and left us, Colman clutching the leaves to his wounds.

"Did Aunt Morag send you?" I asked with curiosity.

"No. She doesn't know I'm here. I wanted to find out how you were." I remembered how all my cousins had thought Juniper was a dangerous witch—I had thought so myself, and even now . . . I realized what a very brave person Colman was.

"She might have cast a spell on you," I said.

"Is it scary?" he asked.

"She's nice." I could not quite bring myself to admit yet that it was great fun living with Juniper, and that I felt as if I had known her all my life.

"What about the jewels?" Colman wanted to know.

"No sign of those," I whispered. "There's an attic that I haven't been into yet. There are two huge cats called Ruby and Pearl—you'll see them, probably—and a broomstick, though so far she's only used it to sweep the floor. Well, *I* swept it, actually. Also, the food's lovely." The excited look faded out of Colman's eyes, and a wistful expression took its place.

"What sort of food?" he asked, and I noticed suddenly how thin he was, even though it was summer—the time when food was easiest to get.

"Milk and stuff," I said carelessly. "Do you want to come and see the house?"

Juniper had disappeared back to her garden, so we were free to wander. I showed him the wonderful carpet with the strange beasts on it, the stones and ornaments, the lute and the harp. I pointed out the mirror over the fireplace.

"It's magic," I told him.

He brushed his hair back with his hand.

"What do you see?" I asked.

"Myself, of course. All mirrors work like that. Nothing magic about that." For the first time in my life with Juniper, the first of many times, I learned that to think something is not necessarily to say it. To have such a secret all of my own made me feel proud, but also a little scared.

Colman loved the carving of the staircase, and touched the silken curtains with a kind of awe. I showed him Juniper's bedroom, the spare bedroom, and the little flight of stairs with the white, ivory-handled door at the top that led into the attic.

When we had done all that, we came down to find that Juniper was taking a pot of stew from the fire. Soon a delicious supper was on the table. Colman, who only five minutes before had been questioning me anxiously about the honey drink, hesitated only a moment. When he saw me pick up my spoon and a piece of bread, he too started to eat with the absolute concentration and rapture with which my cousins always ate, as if there was nothing in the world but food. There was some of Juniper's creamy cheese to follow, and Colman ate a lot of that too. His eyes shone, and his cheeks were as pink as foxgloves.

Eventually we went out into the yard to hunt eggs, and by then Colman felt almost too full to walk. We knew that there should be about twelve eggs—some of them in predictable places where the hens always laid, others much harder to find. Colman climbed the ladder into the hayloft, and there were three eggs up there. Another was in the stable, just where Tillie might step on it.

"Hens are so silly," I grumbled.

"Girls are silly too," said Colman, so I hit him and we

rolled over and over on the ground, fighting and laughing as we had often done before.

As we fell apart, still laughing, I noticed something extraordinary, and pointed. "Look, Colman, your legs!"

Over his knees, where the deep cuts had been, was clean brown skin without a hint of a scar. It was uncanny, and we looked at each other with wide eyes.

"Maybe it's the Devil," said Colman.

We went on looking for eggs, but our birdlike chatter had stopped. Perhaps because I was frightened over what had happened, and was not looking where I was going, I tripped against a rain barrel in the yard and dropped three eggs. Colman looked at me sympathetically.

When we got indoors again, Juniper had arranged a small basket for Colman with some of her own butter and cheese wrapped in grass to keep it cool, a loaf of bread, and sticks of sugared angelica.

"It shouldn't be too heavy walking downhill," she said apologetically.

I could feel Colman hesitating at the thought of taking anything with him from this enchanted house and then see how his mind changed as he thought of all those hungry brothers and sisters at home. How they would crowd around him, eating and talking, eager for all the details of Juniper's house and my new life. I walked with him to the yew hedge, suddenly feeling very homesick as I watched his small figure walk jerkily down the steps, his basket bobbing beside him until he was out of sight.

As if she had known how I would feel, Juniper was sitting waiting for me at the top of the steps. For the first of many times I sat down in her lap, leaning back against her as if it was quite natural to do so.

"He's brave, isn't he?" she said.

"He doesn't think he is. He gets much more frightened than his brothers."

A companionable silence fell between us. There was a luminous greeny-blue sky over the wide view ahead of us. I felt quite unexpectedly happy. I hadn't cried once all day.

"How did you do that thing with his legs and the leaves?" I asked her. "It was a miracle."

"Not really," she said. "Well, no more than anything else. Wounds heal up, don't they, and the scar goes away? Colman's knees would have been better in a few days anyway. That's the real miracle. I just hurried it up a bit."

"How do you do it?"

"Difficult to say. I just kind of concentrate."

"Could I do it?"

"Anyone could do it. If they really wanted to. Most people don't want to."

"I do," I said, thinking what fun it would be to work miracles.

"There's a price to be paid for it, of course," she said. "Well, there is for everything. It's hard work in a way, too."

"Do you mean you wish you didn't do it, then?"

"I'd rather do it than anything in the world."

We sat on quietly for a bit, and then I said, "I had a dream about Finbar today." I was aware of a sudden alertness in Juniper.

"Tell me."

"He was at the helm of a ship, but his back was turned to me. I could not see his face. Why doesn't he come back to take care of me?"

"The voyage has taken hold of him. Voyages do that. He'll be back one day, but maybe not for a while. Meanwhile you've got me to look after you, which is lucky. For both of us."

Leaning back against Juniper's strong, warm body, I felt at peace in a way I had not done since Finbar's big arms had last been around me.

"Are you going to beat me for breaking the eggs?" I asked her sleepily.

"Yes, I expect so," said Juniper, and laughed. I could feel the laugh erupting like a little volcano from right down inside her, and then I began to laugh too and rolled about on Juniper laughing. Tears of laughter came out of my eyes until I had to wipe them away.

"My mother used to beat me," I said. "Then she went away. Maybe because I was so naughty."

"That wasn't the reason, Wise Child." It was comforting to hear her say that, and I did not wonder how she knew.

"Well, why don't you beat me, then?" I was genuinely puzzled.

"I can't be bothered," she said.

"That's no way to bring up a child," I said primly, copying the voices of the village women I knew, and because Juniper began to laugh again, I laughed myself.

"You'll just have to behave yourself, Wise Child," Juniper said. "Or not, as the case may be. I shall never beat you, whatever you do."

"You're a very strange person," I said. "And you've no idea how to bring up children."

"I've got you to teach me," she said.

4

Fairy Food

I WAS TO SEE Colman again quite soon. On Saturday Juniper said "Mass tomorrow!" as if it was the most natural thing in the world. "I thought we'd go down with Tillie, and then I'll wait till it's over and bring you back," she said. "This first time at least."

"I shall have to fast tomorrow morning," I said shyly, not sure how well she understood our customs.

"Of course," she said. "I thought I could bring some bread down, and you can have a bite on the way home. Or a picnic if you'd rather."

I was not sure whether Fillan Priest was glad to see me or not. He greeted me shortly as I entered, and walked me down the aisle with his hand on my shoulder; I was glad to get out from under its weight and scramble over the legs of Conor and Seumas to reach Colman's side. When Fillan gave his exposition of the Gospel, he talked about the powers of darkness and how they must be overcome by the powers of light. Colman, who always listened in church instead of daydreaming as I did, nudged me gently with his elbow.

As if guessing that Fillan might have spoken against her, Juniper asked me about him when I rejoined her. We were walking through a little wood, along the banks of the river, and I was already munching my bread.

"He talked about Pelagius," I lied. Pelagius was an English scholar who had had a quarrel with the great St. Augustine, and Fillan was always defending him or else telling us about the other big quarrel about the date of Easter.

"Pelagius? He who thinks we are good entirely by our own endeavors?" Juniper asked. "The man's a fool."

"Fillan doesn't think so." Truly I did not care one way or another, but I was surprised that Juniper knew about Pelagius.

Although Juniper was not a Christian, from then on Sundays became our holy days, and apart from caring for the animals we did no work. I had soon learned to milk Daisy, and though she never yielded as much milk for me as for Juniper, it was one of my favorite chores; still, I resented having to get up early to do it. On Sundays we would go down to the shore, where Juniper soon taught me to swim, or we would walk in the great meadow, or if it was wet we would light a fire and sit by it and Juniper would tell me her marvelous stories or sing to me. We needed our Sundays, since we worked so hard the rest of the week.

"Pearl shall wake you," Juniper had said a day or two after I had settled in, and every morning the white cat would push the door of the big bedroom open (Juniper had got up long since), jump on my bed, and walk patiently over me until I sat up.

"Go away, Pearl," I would say crossly, but she was persistent and would give me no peace until I got out of bed, ran downstairs, and washed myself in the trough under the cistern in the yard. As I ran in again, shivering and bad-tempered, I could hear Juniper busy in the dairy; I dressed, came downstairs again, and went out to milk Daisy, and by the time I had finished, breakfast was always ready. Then I did some horrible heathen English or worked at astronomy with some of the glass stones on the floor.

That was the easy part. The real labors of the day began in the afternoon. The worst afternoon was one we spent cutting peat—during a period of a waning moon, of course. It was a wet day, when I thought we should have stayed at home by the fire, and the walk to the bog seemed endless. Then I had the job of pulling back the heather roots, which were tough and hurt my hands, to expose the peat underneath. Juniper cut the long, thin pieces of turf with a sharp spade—you push it in at an angle—and then it all had to be piled up in neat heaps to dry. It was boring, backaching work and it took all afternoon before Juniper was satisfied. On another day we would load it all into Tillie's panniers and take it back to the white house, where it would all have to be piled up again.

"Won't that be lovely in the winter!" was Juniper's only comment on our work.

ANOTHER AFTERNOON, nearly as dreadful, we spent collecting sphagnum moss, sundew, and bog myrtle—the first two for whooping cough, which often killed babies in our village, the last to make our winter beer. The sphagnum grew over the wettest places in the bog; once the water and muck came right over the top of my boots and soaked my stockings, and once, trying to save myself from a ducking, I plunged both my hands into the mud. It was very cold, the afternoon was drawing in, and I shivered on the long walk home.

In spite of my coldness and bad temper Juniper made me measure the volume of the myrtle in a tub, take the same amount of water, boil half of it and add honey to it, pour it over the leaves, then add the rest of the water. When it had cooled, I had to add yeast to make it froth. A month later we drank it with our meals, and it tasted good.

In the meantime, however, I was very cross that Juniper would not let me wash or change my clothes until I had completed the whole task, though she *did* have a splendid fire going by the time I had finished.

THERE WERE many days when we walked in search of a root or a leaf, some seeds or a flower, which Juniper needed for some recipe of hers. Other days we hoed and weeded and plucked at home, sometimes laying the herbs out in the sun to dry, sometimes carefully layering them indoors.

I was puzzled that, despite my unwillingness, I still helped. Partly it was because Juniper worked so hard herself, partly it was that in other ways she was so kind to me, and partly it was that she simply took it for granted that I would.

"Plants bore me. Stinking things."

"What's this one?"

"Cow parsley."

"God help us. You'll poison us all yet. It's hemlock, and you can recognize it by its height, by its purple spots, and by the horrid smell it has when it is bruised. Here, smell!"

"Ugh!"

Juniper never scolded me, but she did not reduce either lessons or work. Day after day she repeated names of plants to me, showed me leaves and petals, roots, sap, and seed; made me taste and smell and feel; and day after day she set me, anything but willing, to stir some gruesome-looking green or black mess bubbling in a saucepan over the fire. Hot and almost swooning from the odors, I stirred until my arms felt as if they would drop off.

"Puts me off my dinner," I would grumble, and I would take my food out to eat on the steps.

I hated all the fiddly little processes, the stripping of leaves, the chopping, the crunching of stems. I preferred the milking, and the butter and cheese making, though my arm used to ache from pumping the handle of the churn. (Within a few weeks, though, I noticed that my arms had gotten much stronger, with all the turning and lifting and carrying Juniper required of her assistant.) It was fun to eat the pat of butter or the tiny cheese I had shaped for myself.

"It tastes so much better when you do it yourself," Juniper said.

When we were not busy in the dairy, we were making preserves for the winter, or mashing crab apples to make a spicy drink, or washing our clothes or ourselves. Juniper, unlike my grandmother, was terribly fussy about being clean. She washed me all over once a week out in the yard— it made me scream, the water was so cold—and then she washed my hair with a lotion of rosemary. I could hardly believe it the first time she dried it for me and combed it out. It was black and glistening in the mirror.

"You have lovely hair, Wise Child," she said, and I was really surprised. I did not know that anything about me was lovely. My mother, who was beautiful, had once wondered in my hearing how a woman like her could have a child who looked like me.

I would often study again for an hour or two before suppertime, and by the time I had found the eggs and laid the table and washed the dishes afterward, I was often half asleep in my little green chair. Yet that was often the best part of the day, with Juniper spinning and singing and telling me fairy tales. She had taught me one or two songs and sometimes made me sing them to her.

Colman came again before the week was out, bringing an eel he had caught. He was too little to be as good a fisherman as his brothers; he rarely caught a proper fish, and if he had they would have eaten it at home, but he was good at catching eels. Juniper received him with her usual courtesy, gave him a big doorstep of bread and jam to eat, and told him she hoped he would come again often, as I needed another child to play with. I soon discovered that she would let me off my chores when Colman came.

"Is she still good to you?" he asked when we were alone.

"Of course. Though the herbs are awfully boring. No worse than school, though."

"Your hair looks nice."

"Juniper washed it for me. She says it will be lovely when it grows a bit."

"You don't look so thin either."

"I know." I had noticed that my face had filled out a little and looked both pinker and browner.

"Have you found out anything about the cave yet?"

"Not yet."

craftsman had made that clasp, or he was here with me. It was the oddest feeling, as if time or place might just be an illusion.

"He is making it now," I heard myself say out loud.

I opened the clasp and pushed back the heavy sheets of vellum. Here too was beauty; pictures of the sky by men who had spent whole nights searching it. Like Finbar. I grieved for Finbar at that moment, my head upon my hand.

"Father, come back to me," I said. I could see his wide gaze quite clearly, the gaze of someone who had just heard an unexpected sound. Then his face faded.

When I had finished my astronomy, I turned unwillingly to the herb beds.

"I thought if you were educated you didn't have to do boring things," I had said to Juniper the day before.

"There *are* people who think like that," Juniper had said. "Such a pity. Boredom is so valuable." I could not imagine what she meant.

Perhaps because of the clasp and the vision of Finbar, things were different this morning. The plants, which caused me so much work and trouble, seemed vividly alive in the sunlight. The faces of the marigolds shone with a kind of innocence. I worked steadily among the rows until I got to the back of the garden. The sight of the nightshade and the other sinister plants brought the thought of witchcraft to mind; I was suddenly tempted by the little ivory handle on the attic door. I could go up the stairs and Juniper would never know I had been. Yet suppose I found some of the horrible things witches were said to use in spells—bowls of blood, knives, mutilated animals, skeletons—what should I do then? If Juniper was wicked, she didn't show it to me, and I didn't want her to show it.

Toward twilight I went for a little walk across the meadow. As I passed the stile, I remembered that I had not yet put out the fairy food as Juniper had instructed me; Juniper usually put it out before dark, directly after milking, but surely the fairies did not come till nightfall? I would remember.

I walked in the gloaming along the path Juniper had trodden with her donkey, quietly admiring the great red poppies glowing like fires in the grass. Suddenly I stiffened. There, coming along the path toward me, was Cormac, the horrible Cormac. He had not seen me, clearly was not expecting to see anyone. Even in the half-light I could see his frighteningly swollen and mutilated face, the sores and the swellings, and the appalling eyes surrounded by pus.

Cormac had lived in my nightmares, as in the nightmares of other children in the village. I had particularly hated the thought at Mass that even as we were going to the altar to receive the body of Christ, that hideous, squinting face was spying on us through a window in the church wall. Like all the children, I threw stones at him if I saw him approaching. I did so now. I picked up a rock and hurled it in his direction.

It hit him quite hard on the shoulder, and he gave one yell of total surprise before his eyes fell on me. At once, like a wild animal who has seen a human, he turned and ran. I shuddered with relief.

I went back to the house, finished my chores, left the food out for the fairies, and went to bed.

By the time Pearl woke me the next morning, I could already hear Juniper singing in the dairy.

5

Cormac

YOU WORKED very hard yesterday," Juniper said as I sat down to breakfast. I felt pleased but I didn't want her to know it. I was punishing her for leaving me yesterday.

Presently she went out to feed the hens, and I began to sweep the floor with the hazel broom. She came back with a full pitcher of milk and a cheese in her hands. She looked distressed.

"The fairies did not take their food?" I said in surprise. "Perhaps I was a bit late putting it out."

It was not until lunchtime that I mentioned the leper. "That horrible Cormac was shambling around here. I soon scared him off."

Juniper stared at me with such astonishment that I stared back. "You did *what?*"

"I threw a stone at him," I said virtuously. "I knew you wouldn't want him stealing eggs or staring through the window." (The village women had always said that he stole eggs.)

A look of pain passed across Juniper's cheerful, sunburned face. "I must go and see him," she said suddenly.

"What?"

"I must go and see him. I have been caring for Cormac—for his face, and giving him food—for . . . oh, several years. Only yesterday I brought back some herbs that I thought might help him. Whom do you think I put the food out for every night?"

"For *Cormac*?"

"Of course."

"But he's horrible. All the children throw stones at him. Fillan says that he did something very wicked and he's been punished by getting leprosy."

"Did you know he was Fillan's brother?"

"No. Honestly? But he gives me the shivers. He's disgusting."

"He's sick. And very lonely."

Perhaps because I was so surprised at Juniper's reaction, I could feel my face setting into its most obstinate expression.

"Well, I don't care. I don't want him around here."

"That's a pity. Because we're going to see him."

"When?"

"Now." Even as she spoke, Juniper was moving briskly around the place. She put two baskets on the table. Into one of them she put a big bag of oatmeal, some comfrey, and a small linen bag I had never seen before, presumably the special herb she had brought back with her. Into the other basket she put bread, cheese, oatcakes, milk, and preserves, and covered it all with a clean cloth.

"I'm not coming."

"I need you to help me carry the baskets."

"Tillie can carry them."

"Tillie is not coming. Besides, I want you to come with me."

"I don't want to come."

"Fetch the hairbrush," said Juniper inexorably, and began to brush my hair. "You could put on a clean smock, too."

"For a *leper?*" I asked incredulously.

"Of course. He can see what you look like, can't he?"

Juniper herself changed into a pretty blue dress and put on her new straw hat—not the one with the unraveled bits around the brim.

"I shall wait outside," I said as we began to walk along the track. "I shan't come in. Where does he live, anyway?"

"He has a hut out in the meadow."

It was then that I guessed Juniper must have given him the hut, or at least let him build it, since I knew that most of that land belonged to her. It had not occurred to me before to wonder where Cormac lived once they had turned him out of the village, nor how he could eat when he was always mocked or driven away.

"I don't understand," I said crossly. Juniper did not offer to explain anything; she seemed pretty cross herself.

The sun was warm, Juniper was walking extremely fast, and soon I was sweating with the weight of the basket.

"Is it much farther?" I grumbled. Juniper didn't answer. I shifted the basket from one arm to the other. The flies were buzzing around my hot face. After what seemed a long, long walk, I could see a small cabin in the distance, above the waving blue grass and poppies. As we got nearer, I could see a tiny garden outside it, with a well.

"No smoke," said Juniper, as if to herself, and it was true that there was no sign of a fire or that the cabin was occupied.

"You wait here," Juniper said when we got to the edge of his little garden. Hadn't I already told her that I had no intention of going inside a leper's house? I sat down by the well, and was just going to pull up the cup and give myself a drink of water when I remembered whose lips must have drunk out of that cup, and I let the chain go with a shudder. Juniper walked through the open door of the house, bearing both the baskets. There was no sound. I expected to hear conversation, or that Juniper would come out and tell me that Cormac was away somewhere, but there was silence. It was most odd.

I sat there by the well for a quarter of an hour or so, and then curiosity got the better of me. I walked to the door of the cabin, put my head around it, and there saw Juniper and Cormac. Cormac was sitting upright on a straw pallet on the floor, facing the wall. Somehow I knew he had been weeping. Juniper was sitting on the only chair in the room facing in the same direction as Cormac, and I knew she had not spoken. She was waiting.

I looked around the room, which was simple and orderly. There was the hearth with the smoke hole in the roof, but it was obvious that the ashes were cold and dead and that Cormac had not cooked there recently. Most of the light came through the door and through one opening on the same wall. The earth floor was covered with rushes and herbs that had a sweet smell. There was a wooden chest, one or two books, a shelf that held jars of beans, seeds, nuts. There were some plates, a cup, and cooking pots—a crock

that perhaps held bread. Neither Cormac nor Juniper moved
or spoke, and having looked around the room, I crouched
down on the floor, just inside the door, and wondered what
to do next.

The silence was thick, and within the silence I could feel
Juniper waiting for something, though I could not imagine
what. I sighed, rather loudly, but Juniper did not turn my
way, nor show any sign of having heard me. It struck me
that Cormac, at least seen from the back, did not look as
bad as I had thought. Sitting there on his bed, quite still,
not running away, he looked dignified. All at once I surprised myself with the sound of my own voice.

"I am sorry I threw a stone at you," I said. "I expect I was
frightened." There was another long silence. "It was a silly
thing to do. And I'm sorry you did not take the food. I did
not realize it was for you."

There was still silence in the room, though it felt a
warmer silence. Juniper still waited. Cormac still faced the
wall.

"I'll go outside now," I said. "I don't blame you if you
hate me."

I went outside and again sat by the well, trying to think
what had happened. I had been so sure that I was right to
hate Cormac—hadn't Fillan said that it wouldn't have happened to him if he had not led a wicked life, and that
wicked people ought to be punished? After a few minutes I
could hear voices softly talking inside—I even thought I
heard Juniper laugh, very gently. The voices rose and fell
for a bit, and then Juniper came to the door and said, "Wise
Child, do you think you could find us some firewood?"
Which I did.

Soon the smoke was coming out of Cormac's smoke hole again, and Juniper must have been making a poultice with the oatmeal, because as I crept closer to the door again I could hear her saying, "I hope it's not too hot, but the hotter the better, really." I peeped in, and Juniper was applying the cloths to Cormac's poor face, and Cormac gave only one slight grunt as he felt the heat.

"That's good," said Juniper.

Later on, quite a bit later, she came out to me in the garden and took me by the hand, saying, "Cormac would like to speak to you." I had dreaded having to look Cormac in the face, but since she had me by the hand and I seemed to have caused so much trouble already, I did not know what else I could do but obey. She led me into the hut, and there was Cormac sitting on the chair facing the door. I looked, and looked again in astonishment. In my mind, as in my nightmares, I had always seen Cormac's two ghastly bloodshot eyes, in a yellow, tattered face, horribly alive, the surface of his skin crawling.

I do not know whether it was because Cormac had begun to become real for me or because of the fearlessness and infinite tenderness with which I had seen Juniper touch the living wound, but there was nothing there that frightened me now; just two sad dark eyes, one whole cheek, most of a nose, and another cheek raw and whitened and pitted with holes.

I looked carefully—there seemed nothing else to do. "It's not as bad as I thought," I blurted out. A ghost of a smile seemed to cross Cormac's features.

"I'm glad," he said, in his poor, thickened speech. "Perhaps I won't scare you so much."

"I'm no longer scared of you, sir," I said, and I meant it.

I kept searching for whatever it was that had frightened me before.

Juniper and I walked silently home. After supper, a silent supper, when we had washed the dishes, we sat in our chairs without stories or singing.

"Are you angry with me?" I asked at last. Without speaking, Juniper held out her arms, and I climbed into her comfortable blue lap and leaned against her.

"I didn't know he was . . . like that," I said at last. "Fillan said he had committed a terrible sin and that was how God had punished him."

"Fillan may hate Cormac, but I don't think God does," said Juniper. "Your God loves people, doesn't he? Jesus healed the lepers, and he forgave people who did wrong, even the ones who crucified him. Isn't that right? So why would he give Cormac—dear good Cormac—such a dreadful punishment? What could he possibly have done that was bad enough?"

"Fillan didn't say. I suppose he could have killed somebody," I said speculatively. "Or done something wicked with his body, like, you know . . ."

"Lots of people kill other people without getting leprosy," said Juniper, "as well as hurting them in all sorts of other ways. Of course, it does sometimes make them ill in their minds, and their minds sometimes make their bodies ill, but usually we don't know why people are ill."

"What about your medicine? Will it make Cormac well? Like the cuts on Colman's legs?"

"I don't know. It's more difficult. Maybe Fillan's hatred makes it harder to get well. Maybe my medicine is not strong enough. But I expect it is."

There was a long, easy silence between us.

"You know," I said at last, "I thought the plants were just boring and silly. Fussing around with leaves and roots and seeds. I didn't think they could really change anything. Now . . . it makes it worth the effort."

Juniper laughed. "They're part of the energy . . . the pattern. You'll see one day."

As if the conversation had started the train of thought, I said, "I saw Finbar yesterday. In my mind, you know."

"Yes?"

"I told him to come back. He acted surprised, as if he had forgotten and had to be reminded."

"Mmm . . ." said Juniper. "Sounds like Finbar."

6

Flying

SEPTEMBER was a golden month. My hair grew longer, my face, which had looked so white and pinched, was rosy, and I kept being surprised at how well and glad I felt, at how much energy I had.

"I'm different now, aren't I?" I said to Juniper, who smiled.

We went on blackberrying expeditions just as I had done with my cousins; we also collected cloudberries and blueberries, wineberries and elderberries, cowberries and red currants, hindberries and barberries, sloes and rose hips, crowberries and guelder-rose berries, hazelnuts and sweet chestnuts, the last of which meant going to a very secret place Juniper knew where there was a single tree. I liked picking berries, not least because you could eat as you worked. My face was usually stained with juice that autumn. We also went to the shore several times and collected as much driftwood as Tillie could carry. We made a big pile of it in the yard. Juniper produced some thick woven ma-

terial and began to make me a cloak. We were getting ready
for the winter.

The days were shorter and darker, and about midday we
would light our fire. Milking Daisy in the late afternoons,
I found my hands were cold and I was glad to run back into
the house. We came back from our food-collecting expeditions with mud weighting our shoes.

Juniper had started to teach me Latin.

"We will have more time for study when winter comes,"
she told me. Juniper was a wonderful teacher, partly because lessons got mixed in with everything else. She would
draw a picture of the seas and countries around Britain so
that I would understand the story of a voyage or a love story
or a battle, and she would alternate a piece of history with
a fairy story so that my attention remained sharp. I puzzled
over what was "real."

"Did that *really* happen?" I would ask Juniper. "Or is it
just a story?"

"*Just* a story," she would echo me mockingly.

"Are fairies real?" I asked her once.

"Of course," she said unhesitatingly.

"Well, why can't I see them?"

"There are many kinds of reality," Juniper explained.
"Only silly people think there is only one kind. I don't live
in the fairy reality and neither do you. I live in two or three
kinds of reality, though. So, I expect, will you."

She did not explain this, even when I begged her to. She
could be quite obstinate about the things she would, and
would not, talk about. "I might spoil something for you,
you see," she said.

One day she said casually, "Euny's coming soon."

"Who's Euny?" I asked.

"Euny looked after me when I was a bit older than you. A bit like the way I look after you."

"Is she a witch too?"

"If you want to put it like that, yes."

"Was she kind to you?"

"In a rather odd way, yes. I owe her my life, among other things."

Even I was silenced by that, as also by the feeling that Juniper was struggling for words to tell me something else.

"Do you trust me, Wise Child?"

"Of course." So completely had Juniper captivated me that I found it difficult to believe I had ever been afraid of her.

"Would you trust me if I told you to do something you really hated? That scared you?"

"Why would you do that to me?"

"Because you would be glad afterward. It would be very good for you. Only you wouldn't know that at the time, and I probably couldn't explain it to you."

"I don't know," I said.

THIS WAS a rather disturbing conversation. Another disturbing conversation was one I had with Colman. We were lying out in the hayloft as usual—we played sieges there, with one of us being the attacker and the other the defender, swiping each other with bundles of hay. When we were tired, we pulled the hay over ourselves to keep warm and talked of all sorts of things—my life with Juniper, his life in the village.

"Maeve the Fair wants to see you," he said suddenly.

"What?" My heart turned over, with a feeling that might have been joy or might have been terror.

"I heard Gregor and Morag talking. Gregor always liked Maeve, Morag told me. Maeve has been on at him to let her see you. Morag was against it."

"Where *is* Maeve?" It had not occurred to me to ask that question in years. It was as if she had dropped off the earth itself when she left me.

"She has a house on the island and another on the mainland. She is rich, you know, because many men love her." Colman paused.

"My mother thought she should not see you. That you had settled down with Juniper and that you should stay here until Finbar comes back. Gregor couldn't see the harm. They didn't know that I was listening, of course. But I thought that you should be the one to choose."

How could I choose? I could scarcely remember Maeve. I only knew I was afraid of her.

"Do you want to see Maeve?" Colman asked.

"I don't know," I whispered. I pushed the conversation down into the dark places of my mind and did not even tell Juniper about it.

THE NEXT DAY Juniper and I went into the garden and started plucking the leaves of the henbane and the seeds of the thorn apple.

"I thought we weren't supposed to touch these," I said, disliking the smell of the henbane.

"As I said—there's a right time for everything," said Juniper.

"How do you know that Euny's coming?" I asked her as

we chopped up the leaves and pounded the seeds in the mortar. "There's an awful lot of this stuff—whatever is it we're making?"

"A sort of ointment. I just know, that's all."

In half an hour a most awful smell filled the house, and I opened the door to let it out. Even the cats, who had begun to stay indoors a lot since the weather had turned colder, fled to the barn.

"It's disgusting!" I complained.

"You're all likes and dislikes," said Juniper, as if I was being entirely unreasonable. I privately thought that anyone would have disliked that smell, which was like stagnant ponds and rotten meat and stale sweat, as well as being cloyingly sweet at the same time.

If I hoped Juniper might tell me to run along and play, I was wrong. After the cauldron had boiled and bubbled for a couple of hours, she sent me to fetch some beeswax; she placed the beeswax in a big bowl, softened it over the steam of the cauldron, and then, a little at a time, began to stir the greeny-black fetid liquid into the beeswax. Eventually there was in the bowl a brownish ointment, which smelled of wax now as well as the herbs, and she seemed satisfied.

"Thank goodness, that's done," I said, "though I can't imagine anyone would use something that smelled like that."

Euny arrived toward the end of the afternoon, a tiny old woman dressed in black. From the moment she appeared I could not take my eyes off her, trying to see what Juniper had liked so much about her, and how she might have saved Juniper's life. She was wrinkled, white-haired, and scrawny, and had lost several teeth. Her voice had a grating quality, and she smelled of something I didn't like much—garlic? mint? cloves? It seemed to be a mixture of all of them. What I couldn't get used to was that she called Juniper by her real Cornish name of Ninnoc.

"So this is the child?" she said, staring at me critically as I stood and wriggled in front of her, hating being looked at as if I was a horse or a dog. "She doesn't carry much weight," she said at last.

"She's quite fat compared to what she used to be," said Juniper. "And she gets prettier and prettier." I knew I wasn't *very* pretty, but it made me feel better that Juniper liked the way I looked.

"Is she useful around the house?" Euny asked.

Juniper, who liked to be truthful, considered a moment.

"She tries very hard," she said at last. "And she's a good scholar."

"Huh!" said Euny, and I could tell she didn't think much of book learning.

I decided I didn't like Euny much even if she had saved Juniper's life, and I crept out to the barn and talked to Daisy for a bit. When it got too cold, I went back into the house and slipped noiselessly past them and up the stairs to Juniper's bedroom and my own bed, but they were so busy talking they scarcely noticed me. *I* might not like Euny, but to Juniper she was clearly special.

When I judged it was getting near suppertime, I crept out onto the landing, meaning to go downstairs. Juniper and Euny seemed to be disagreeing about something.

"She's very young," Juniper was saying.

"Old enough," said Euny.

"I wish we needn't."

"You think it's a kindness. It isn't."

I knew that they were talking about me, and I didn't like the sound of it. I coughed a little so that they would know I was coming, and I walked downstairs.

"I thought perhaps supper would soon be ready," I said coldly to Juniper.

"There won't *be* supper tonight," Juniper said gently.

"None?" I said disbelievingly.

"No. I'll explain why later."

I was shocked, hurt, angry. We *always* had supper, and I was hungry. If I'd known sooner, I would have eaten more at teatime. To show how offended I was, I went back upstairs, and then, feeling very sad, I climbed into bed without undressing and pulled the bedclothes over me. I lay there for a while, hearing the voices rising and falling downstairs in what seemed to be an argument, and then, because I was quite tired from all the work involved in getting ready for Euny, I fell asleep.

Hours later, it seemed, a hand clutched my shoulder, and I woke up in fright.

"Get up!" said Euny's voice, not unsympathetically. "Come downstairs."

"What for?" I asked, trying to still a feeling of terror in my heart.

"Don't ask questions. Ninnoc will tell you."

I got up with a heavy heart and shuffled to the stairs, stony with sleep. Downstairs Juniper had prepared a bath for me in front of the fire; I thought she must have gone mad.

"Take off your clothes, Wise Child," she said heavily.

"In front of Euny?" I said incredulously. My people did

not let others see them naked very much. Juniper nodded. She looked unusually pale and tired, I noticed, not her usual rosy and cheery self. Very slowly I stripped off my smock and the shift I wore beneath it, and stepped into the warm water with an ominous sense of strangeness. You did not wake people up in the middle of the night to give them baths, particularly when you'd forgotten to give them any supper.

Juniper lifted me out of the water into the big, fluffy cloth she always used to wipe me dry after a bath, and for a moment, warm and in her arms, I thought maybe everything was all right, but then I felt a stiffening in her body and was aware that over my shoulder her eyes were fixed on something.

I glanced around quickly, and there was Euny coming toward us, staggering under the big bowl of beeswax and herbs. I shrank toward Juniper, uncertain of what was going to happen.

"Wise Child," said Juniper, and she seemed to have a catch in her throat, "it is necessary for us to use the ointment. As a way of showing you something. I know you won't like the idea, but bear with us. We won't hurt you."

I didn't speak, because I could not for the life of me think what they were going to do with the stuff. What they did was stand me on the cloth in front of the fire, and then both of them dipped their hands into the foul mess in the bowl and advanced toward me. They started smearing it on my naked body.

"No!" I yelled as I realized what they intended to do, and caught the disgusting whiff of the ointment all over again.

"Be patient, Wise Child," said Juniper in her gentlest voice.

"Hold still, child," Euny said crossly. By now they were covering my legs, my thighs, my heels, even the soles of my feet. It felt disgustingly greasy. Soon it was all over my arms, my hands—I could see myself in the mirror as a tiny brown figure with an anguished white face at the top. But then Euny seized my hair and started rubbing the stuff, not at all gently, into my scalp and into my ears. My hair stood up in greasy tufts, but soon that too was covered with the slimy ointment and stuck like a cap to my head. Meanwhile, Juniper, very gently, was smearing the stuff across my forehead, my chin, my cheeks, my nose, and all around my eyes. She was careful not to get it into my eyes, but it scarcely mattered. The terrible stench of it made them smart and water. Juniper and Euny laid the cloth on my little green chair and advised me to sit down, and in utter misery I did so.

I felt ravaged, desolate beyond words, as if my body was hateful, an enemy to me; I was a tiny knot of misery and wretchedness.

Angry and frightened as I was, I somehow could not stop myself from turning to Juniper, trying to seek some clue in her face about the hateful thing that had overtaken me. She sat very close beside me, looking at me with great tenderness, and I tried to tell her what I was feeling.

"I don't understand," I said to her, weeping, and I could see it cut her to the heart. But there was no time for more conversation. As my warm body melted some of the ointment, the stench grew intolerable and I could feel the sickness rising from my empty stomach. Broken with faintness and nausea, I leaned my head against the arm of Juniper's chair, too ill now to wonder or do anything but helplessly surrender.

Suddenly I thought I saw something out of the corner of my eye, and turned my head quickly. It was as if a piece of the roof had come right off, and I could see the sky and the stars through it. I sat up and stared hard at it, aware of both Juniper and Euny watching me intently. Then there was more of the sky—I could see that the roof had now rolled all the way back—and shining there in the heavens was the huge orange hunter's moon. I was no longer aware now of the stench, nor of the greasy clutch of the ointment—I realized suddenly that I was weightless, that I was beginning to move upward.

"Wait a moment, Wise Child!" Juniper shouted to me, grabbing me by the hand. She walked across the room holding on to me—I half flew across the floor—and she bent and handed me the hazel broom. I jumped astride it. I also heard her say, "Go, Pearl!" Pearl leaped onto the handle of the broom, Juniper let go, and I flew up, up, up into the luminous, moon-filled sky. I managed to seat myself quite comfortably on the fatter part of the broom; Pearl crouched at full length, facing the way we were going, directing us. I was high, high up, high over the house and the cliff and the meadow and the bog and the village. I could see Cormac's little hut in the meadow, brilliant in the moonlight, and I could see the sea away in the distance with a path of moonbeams riding upon it. I noticed that the roof seemed to be back on Juniper's house again. I did not feel at all cold. Then, as if gathering speed, the broom turned sharply and headed for the sea and the mainland. Soon I was passing the huge peaks, and I could see the crevices and corries, the valleys in steep rock faces, perfectly clearly. Beneath us was what I knew to be the Great Glen, with its necklace of lochs.

We flew on for some minutes, and then we were over the sea again. It was colder now, but the air was deliciously fresh upon me. My skin shone white in the moonlight, without any trace of the brown ointment that had disfigured it. Pearl glowed brightly ahead of me, the moon irradiating her brilliant fur. Once or twice I thought I heard her speak to me, but decided I must have imagined it. I was trying desperately to remember what Juniper had taught me in her geography lessons. What was it that lay on the far side of that cold sea? I could not remember.

Soon, however, I began to see a group of islands below us and realized that the broom was going down. It traveled at quite a steep angle, and I felt indignant that if I had not sensibly been holding on tight, I might have fallen off. At once, though, I remembered Juniper's laughing remark to me on the way home from the day at the bog.

"You always feel someone must be to blame when you are cold or miserable or frightened, Wise Child. It may not be so at all—it is just the weather of life—but even if they are to blame . . . does it matter?"

The island on which we were coming down was a mountainous place. I could see a circle of stones, with another avenue of stones leading up to them. The broomstick dropped me at the end of the avenue farthest from the circle. It was odd to feel my bare feet on cold turf, and for a moment I was dizzy from the flying. Then Pearl set off ahead of me, at a dignified pace, waving her tail high in the air. Leaving the broom on the ground, I followed her.

The stones were huge in the moonlight. There seemed to be total silence, as if the living creatures were intently watching, and the moon was very large, bigger than I ever remembered it. I found myself trying to match the quietness around me, putting my feet down on the wet grass as carefully as if I was stalking a wild beast, but what filled me was a sense of enormous reverence. Fillan had once told me how the Christians, in times past, walked to the altar barefoot to receive the sacrament. What sacrament was I about to receive? All my senses were very sharp. I was aware of the scent of the plants and the grasses I crushed beneath the soles of my feet, of the air gently touching my naked body, of the blood pulsing in and out of my heart, of the passage of food far down in my belly.

At once I knew that the movement of the blood within me was part of the same pattern that moved the sap in the oak tree to my right. The decay of the food in my stomach was the same as the autumn decay of the plants and trees. When Juniper and I shoveled earth upon our human droppings, I knew that the flies and the little earth creatures fed upon them; this was their food as the fish and animals and roots and berries and seeds were ours. I began to weep at the beauty of this, to say a psalm that Fillan had once taught me praising the good God.

I was now emerging from the avenue and into a circle of much bigger stones, which made me feel as tiny as an ant. I also felt very dignified, like someone walking in a procession. I walked even more slowly, over the short, tussocky grass; Pearl led me on through this outer circle and through two concentric inner ones, and at last the two of us were in a clearing with one flat stone in the middle of it like an altar. Pearl walked ahead of me to this stone, and there she stopped and the two of us stood side by side. I felt nonplused.

"What do you want of me?" I asked the altar stone at

last. I was not very surprised when it didn't reply, though I asked the question three times. All the same, I knew that one day that place would teach me the answer.

I stood there for a bit, I suppose praying is the word for what I was doing—to God, to Christ, to that special, magic place, to the wild world about me, to St. Brigid, St. Michael, to Columba, to Finbar, to Juniper, my most intimate saints. I was roused from this reverie by Pearl brushing herself gently against my legs. I looked behind me, in the direction in which she was facing, and I could see what looked like a shiny ball, approaching us down the avenue about two feet from the ground. Only when it reached the last of the stone circles did I recognize it for what it was—Juniper's broom. It circled me several times as if impatient to be off, and at last I realized that I had to run to catch up with it and jump upon it. Pearl and I jumped at the same moment, and the broom at once shot upward in its sudden, inconsiderate way (once again I felt very cross and wanted to blame somebody), and we made our way into the great arc of the sky.

As if the business of the evening was over, I thoroughly enjoyed the ride back, feeling the wind running through my hair, noticing the autumn constellations, which seemed to be very close, the cheese moon, the luminosity of the sky, which was not dark at all but patched with different colors of light. Nearer to home I noticed the branches of trees, which had a strange jewel quality, and the grass of the meadow surging softly like a sea beneath me.

Then, with a shock that made my head spin, I was sitting in my little green chair with Juniper and Euny seated beside me, and the disgusting smell of the ointment in my nostrils, and the roof back on the house.

"Come!" said Juniper with her old certainty and briskness. "I'm going to give you another bath." In fact, two baths were waiting beside the hearth.

I was cold and shivering, so I was glad to have Juniper help me into the first of the baths—I stumbled and fell like a drunken man. She carefully washed away the filthy ointment and bathed my sticky hair. This took quite a lot of work. Then she lifted me clear from one bath to the other— Euny bore away the first bath and that terrible smell with it—and this bath was full of sweet-smelling herbs, and here the last traces of the ointment were washed away. Juniper wrapped me in a clean cloth and dried me on her lap, and then carried me, big girl as I was, up the stairs and placed me in her own bed. I was so sleepy that I only faintly knew it when she eventually climbed into bed beside me, and I did not wake again until morning.

7

The Attic

I WOKE UP the next morning knowing that something extraordinary had happened, and saw Juniper sitting, smiling, in a chair beside the bed.

"Well!" she said.

"Well!" I said.

"I should stay in bed for a bit if I were you. You may feel a bit dizzy if you try to get up."

"I'm hungry."

"Good. You shall have your breakfast right away."

"Where's Euny?"

"Oh, she's gone."

"That was a short visit."

"She did what she came to do."

It was only after I had eaten my breakfast gruel and had slept a bit more that I dared to ask Juniper, "What happened?"

"You tell me," she said. "Then I will tell you what I know."

"It seemed to me that the roof was rolled back and that I flew. Only when I came to myself downstairs, I wondered if I had just dreamed it, and it hadn't really happened at all."

"Never mind about that now," she said. "What happened when you flew?"

"I flew like anything. It was a lovely feeling. I managed to sit on the broom, with Pearl sitting on the handle in front of me, and we flew first of all over the meadow and Cormac's house, then back here again (the roof was on again by now) and over the village and the sea and the mainland. Then we came to mountain peaks and forests and what I think was the Great Glen. Then over the sea again."

Juniper was listening with great concentration. "Yes?"

"The broomstick came down on an island. It was at the foot of an avenue of enormous stones. Everything was—oh, so beautiful. Partly it made me feel very little, but partly it made me feel—you know, sort of part of it all. I passed through one stone circle, then another, with Pearl walking in front of me, and then I came to a tiny circle with an altar in the middle of it."

"Then?"

"Then I asked the altar what it wanted of me three times—I walked around it widdershins. There was no answer, and then the broomstick came rushing up the avenue to fetch me and I came away."

Juniper had looked very thoughtful through this long recital.

"So what does it mean?" I asked her, propped up on my elbow in bed. Even that slight movement made my head buzz in a funny way, so I soon lay down again.

"It was a way of seeing if you are . . . one of us."

"One of you and Euny? You mean—a witch?"

"That's just a vulgar word for it that can mean all kinds of things. The word we use is *doran*." Juniper went on to explain that the word *doran* came from our Gaelic word *dorus*, an entrance or way in (the English have a word very like it). It was someone who had found a way in to seeing or perceiving.

"Seeing or perceiving what?"

Juniper hesitated. "The energy," she said at last. "The pattern."

I did not know what she meant, but I knew what interested me.

"Am I a *doran* then?" I asked breathlessly.

"You could be," she said. "You may be one day if . . . various things work out that way."

"So what does a *doran* do, then?"

"Some of us do healing things, like me and my herbs. Some of us sing, or write poetry or make beautiful things. Some don't *do* anything at all. They often stay in one place, and they just *know*."

"*Know?* Know what?"

"How things are," said Juniper mysteriously.

"I didn't like it much last night," I said, changing the subject. "To start with, that is. I hated all that stuff with the ointment, and you wouldn't let me have any supper and Euny was all cross and bossy."

"It was the only way to do it, Wise Child. I couldn't explain any of it to you in advance—otherwise you would be *expecting* things instead of finding them out for yourself, and you know how I hate that. And you had to do it fasting, or

you would have felt much iller than you did. All the same"—
she grinned—"I nearly lost my nerve, and if Euny hadn't
been here I probably would have. That's why she came."

"I'm glad she did, then. The frightening bit was that I
thought you had turned against me."

"Yes, that was the hardest thing. For me, too."

I was thoughtful for a while.

"Did Euny ever give you a test like that?"

"Of course. We were in Brittany at the time. I flew
farther than you. I flew all the way here—that is how I knew
that one day this would be where I would live and work.
And Euny too once went through that test when she was a
little girl in Cornwall. Every *doran* has gone through it."

"But it might not have worked?"

"No. You might just have sat there, getting crosser and
crosser and hating me more and more."

"But you thought I would fly?"

"Yes, I had that sort of feeling about you—a feeling that
the cards confirmed, by the way—the first time I ever saw
you, just as Euny had the feeling the first time she ever saw
me—playing in the sea in Cornwall. But you need to be
quite sure, you see. Flying is the infallible test."

"That you will become a *doran?*"

"No. Only that you have it in you to become one. You
may decide later that you don't want to, or circumstances
may somehow prevent you."

"What circumstances?"

"Things happen," said Juniper.

"And if I decide to become one, then will I end up living
on that island?"

"At Brodgar? Not necessarily. It is just an indication that

that place is of great importance in your life. We don't yet know in what way."

"Well, I think I'll decide to become a *doran* now."

"You can't. You just have to wait and see."

I FELT very tired that day after all the excitement of flying. When I sat up, the room spun around me, and my legs, as they touched the floor, felt as if they were made of sponge. By crawling on my hands and knees, I reached the chair where my clothes were laid out, and without attempting to stand up again, I put them on. I pulled myself into a standing position with the help of the chair, groped my way to the door, trying to ignore the way the floor rose and fell like the deck of a ship, and outside the door I once again crawled to the head of the stairs. There was only one way to negotiate the stairs, and that was to turn around and go down them backward like a tiny child, feeling for them with my feet. When I got to the bottom, I found Juniper watching this performance sympathetically.

"This first day's the worst," she said. "Tomorrow you will feel a lot better, and the day after as if nothing unusual had happened to you." She gave me her arm to help me to my chair, which felt like a safe anchorage. I was all right as long as I kept perfectly still, but any movement, however slight, started the horrible feeling of vertigo. It was going to be a long, boring day. My head ached, and I suddenly felt so tired of my body that I wiped away a tear. Juniper noticed it at once.

"Could you bear a potion?" she asked. "If I gave you some of my very best tea afterward to take away the taste? It would make you feel a lot better."

I nodded miserably, a movement which started the buzzing and vertigo again. She was right, though. The potion took the headache away, and the tea took away the awful taste of it. But I was still too dizzy to stand up. Juniper stopped work early that day, took me on her lap, and sang to me. I felt less like a future *doran* than like a very little girl who needed to be cuddled.

"You know when I left this room and started to fly? What was funny was that I didn't seem to have the ointment on me anymore, though as soon as I got back, there it was again. Did I *really* fly or not? Could you and Euny see me while I was gone?"

"*Really*," Juniper said, smiling. "Didn't I tell you there were many kinds of reality? When the ointment began to have an effect on you, then you were in one kind of reality and Euny and I were in another. So yes, we could see you here while you were on the trip."

"So it wasn't real?" I said, disappointed.

"Remember how you felt up there in the sky, or walking up the stone avenue, or standing in front of the altar? Was that less real than sitting here now and talking?"

"Maybe more real," I said. "Certainly more interesting."

"Well, there," she said.

By the time I woke up the next morning, I was already a lot better, though once again Juniper did not send Pearl to wake me and I slept late. I no longer felt tired, and when I got out of bed and walked experimentally around the room, I was still a bit dizzy but the floor only rocked a little, as if the rough sea beneath it had subsided. I could feel an idea bubbling away energetically at the back of my mind, and at first I could not imagine what it was. Some-

"I do like it in here," I said.

"Good. Come as often as you like."

"You don't mind?"

"Not a bit. In fact I knew you'd soon decide to come."

"What's it for, then, the weaving?"

"Look at it. The colors. What does it remind you of?"

I looked long and hard at the weaving, staring at it from various angles, turning my head on one side to see how it looked then. I kept getting the feeling I had had when I first saw it, that it reminded me of something, but I still couldn't think what it was.

"I don't know," I said at last. "What is it?" Juniper didn't reply. She had that way of not answering you, yet not seeming rude or nasty the way other people do when they won't reply.

"When I first came here," I told her, "I thought the attic might be full of . . . horrible things, like my cousins said. But it isn't. It's lovely."

THE NEXT MORNING I felt perfectly normal, just as Juniper had said I would. In fact life seemed boringly humdrum after the thrill of my flight and of wondering whether I was destined to be a *doran*.

"Why is everything so dull?" I grumbled.

"*I* think the dull bits are often the best," Juniper said. "Too much excitement is very distracting. You just need it now and then to give you something to feed off."

I didn't think I needed it just now and then. I wanted a lot of it. The next day, however, there was a sort of excitement I didn't enjoy at all.

I was going down the cliff to Mass as on so many Sundays, and although Juniper did not always come with me, on this occasion she did because there was a sick old lady she wanted to visit. As we reached the bottom of the cliff path, we had to cross the plank bridge over the stream. I had never liked crossing it much, because there was no handrail and halfway across you seemed a long way from either bank, and if you looked down you could see the water running underneath in a way I did not like. Tillie did not like it much either, and Juniper had always had to lead her. I had followed behind, feeling scared but not too scared. This morning, however, the water was running much more quickly than usual. The streams high up in the mountains had come pouring down into our little stream, and probably some snow had melted up on the height and the water was leaping and frothing and bubbling, making a loud noise and occasionally making boulders bound as it tore along.

Juniper walked ahead of me as usual, leading Tillie, but she did not notice until she got to the farther bank that I had stuck in the middle. I had looked down and had become rooted to the spot, paralyzed with fear. Unable to remain upright, I had dropped to my knees, as I had when I was dizzy after flying, my hands clinging desperately to the planks on each side of the bridge.

Juniper flung Tillie's reins over a branch, came back, lifted me bodily—she managed to do this in a quite gentle way—and carried me to the farther bank, where she set me down. We walked on toward the church, neither of us referring to what had happened. When I had left her, however, and was inside the church at my prayers, my skin grew prickly with horror at the thought that I would have to cross that bridge again in order to get home. I could not imagine how I could do it.

Juniper was waiting, as usual, outside the church, and

the two of us, with Tillie, set off immediately toward the bridge. As if both of us were aware of an ordeal ahead, neither of us spoke at all. Usually I chattered, with Juniper occasionally throwing in an interesting sentence or two. When we got to the bridge, Juniper behaved as if the morning's scene had not occurred. She walked ahead with Tillie, and it was only when she reached the far side that she looked around to see if I was following her. I wasn't—in fact, I had not even set foot on those trembling planks. If I thought that she would come back and carry me this time, I was mistaken. She sat down on a log on the other side of the stream with the air of someone who was prepared to wait for a long time. Quite sure that there was no way I would ever cross that bridge unless Juniper carried me, I too sat down—on a rock—and prepared for a long wait.

Time began to pass very slowly indeed as I thought of the various possibilities. One possibility was that I might simply die of cold. It was not a *very* cold day, but it was quite bad enough, and I longed to be back at home by the fire. Also I was getting hungry. Juniper had given me my usual slice of bread outside the church—I remembered with pleasure that I had not eaten all of it and spent a happy few minutes finishing the rest—but I knew that a chicken stew awaited me at the top of the cliff. There seemed no possible way of getting there, and if Juniper was not prepared to carry me, or even prepared to bring me a bit of stew from her own dinner, then I could not imagine what was to become of me.

No one could have lived with Juniper as long as I had without getting into the habit of pondering the why of things. As the minutes passed and nothing happened, I began to ask myself why it was that today I was so frightened. I had crossed that bridge many, many times, always with a slight quiver of fear but never paralyzed with the horror of it as I was today.

Suddenly the truth came to me. It was the dizziness of the flying that was still troubling me. But that made no sense either. The dizziness had gone two days ago, and I could walk as well as ever. Yes . . . but . . . the helpless feeling I had had when I was dizzy had brought up some much more frightened feeling in me, the feeling I had always pushed down when I crossed this bridge. It was a terror of falling, of being lost and swept away, of losing myself, of not being Wise Child anymore.

As if a door had opened, I suddenly thought of something else. Only the other night, on my flying trip, as I had walked up the great stone avenue, I had felt part of everything, part of animal and bird, tree and stone. If I was part of everything, then I was also part of bridge and stream, of the sharp rocks beneath the water and the tumbling, rushing waters. *Even* if I fell into the waters, and *even* if I was swallowed up by them, I would still be a part of it all. In such a world, such a universe, nothing terrible could happen to me.

Suppose, I asked myself, just suppose that I walked across that bridge as if I was part of it and part of the water, that I decided that whatever happened as I did so, it would be all right, what then? Suddenly it was as if a weight had dropped off me. I stood up, walked to the bridge, and crossed it with only the slightest hesitation as I got to the middle. Juniper stood up as I reached the far bank, gave me one loving, comprehending smile, picked up Tillie's reins, and started for home. One part of me felt very relieved and rather proud. Another part missed the thrill of being terrified; it had been exciting in a way. How muddling everything always was.

8

Temptation

THE WINTER DAYS were upon us. Each morning Juniper lit a fire in the big room and Ruby and Pearl sat one on each side of it like statues. I no longer had to wash myself in the yard but each evening carried water up to my nest in a jug and washed the next morning from a bowl. It was getting cold in the house, and I didn't wash any more than Juniper made me.

I was getting better and better at my lessons. I could write well now, mostly because of practice. I wrote down poems and recipes. Sometimes I opened Juniper's big books about plants and spells, and because I was now learning Latin, I could read a word here and there.

What was nice about the colder days was that we both had more time. Instead of walking the fields or working in the garden until my legs ached, we were often at home now in the afternoons. Juniper was still busy, spinning and sewing—and making me, unenthusiastic about it as ever, spin and sew too. We also did some dyeing in wonderful greens and reds, using herbs instead of seaweed. I enjoyed that. Somehow the winter rhythm of our work felt relaxed and easy—there no longer were flowers or berries to gather, nor roots to dig now that the ground was frozen, and only a very few seeds left to collect. More and more we sat by the fire and talked.

Juniper told me some amazing stories—stories about Cornwall and Ireland and Dalriada in the olden days, stories about the Dragon of Beinn Fhada who got impaled by a hero on a spiked jetty because he was so greedy, and Ossian whose mother was a hind, and Etain who was turned by her jealous stepmother into a scarlet fly; there was the naughty hero Cu Chulainn, and the giantess Binne-bheul, who sang so beautifully that the birds and beasts stopped to listen to her. Every year she plunged herself into the sea to renew her youth, but one year she did not do so and died of old age. My favorite stories, however, were about Tir-nan-Og, the isles of eternal youth. Some people claimed they could see the isles in the western sea at sunset, but I had no idea how to get to them. Juniper said that when people reached them and walked in the marvelous palaces, it happened by a sort of accident, not because they were trying especially. Manannan, the king of the isles, would withdraw his cloak of invisibility only for people he particularly favored—it might be for a poor fisherman or a farmer's boy, a milkmaid or a prince. When they reached the isles, however, all their problems were solved—they knew how they should live their lives in the future. I hoped so much that Manannan would decide to favor me.

Now that the days were shorter, I was slower and sleepier—as Juniper said, like a little mole just beginning to hibernate. This was partly because of the coming of winter, I suppose, but also because I had relaxed into life in Juniper's house as if being there was the most natural thing in the world. All the strain of the last months had drained away; I was in a safe place and could rest in it.

"When Maeve left, where did she go?" I asked Juniper once. Somehow I had never dared ask anyone that question.

"South to England," she said. "A man from Northumbria took her away."

"But I was her little girl. She should have stayed here with me."

Juniper would not say yes or no to this, but looked at me with her wide, clear gaze.

"Maybe it was better as it was."

I was remembering something, something I did not want to remember: the amulets in my mother's room, a queer sort of doll I had found hidden there that Maeve smacked me for playing with, something peculiar in a jar, some liquid I had once seen her pour into a guest's food.

"Was my mother a *doran*?"

"No."

"A witch, then?"

Juniper hesitated again. "She did magic," she said at last. "I think for herself."

"Did Finbar like her doing magic?"

"By the time he knew, it was too late." I thought I detected a sort of bitterness in her voice. "She was amazingly beautiful, you know. It . . . confused . . . people."

Suddenly there was something I needed to know, but it was painful to ask.

"Am I beautiful?"

"No," said Juniper calmly.

"Ugly, then?"

"No." She laughed. "Certainly not. You're going to look lovely."

IN DECEMBER we woke to frost drawings on the windows and I shivered my way down to breakfast. Juniper produced an enormous black fur from a cabinet—a bear's coat, she said it was—and placed it on my bed at night as I lay in my nest; I loved to stroke it with my hands before I went to sleep.

"I have to go away soon," Juniper said one day. "For three days."

Suddenly I felt very small and afraid.

"Who will light the fire?" I asked in a small voice.

"You will. It's quite easy."

I could not speak because of the lump in my throat.

"What will I do when I'm afraid of the dark?" I asked her shamefacedly at last.

"You will wrap yourself in your bear's coat and you won't be afraid," she said.

I wanted to shout and stamp and say that I was too small to be left for so long, that she was bad to do it to me, that she would go away as Maeve had done and I would never see her again, but instead I was dumb and desolate. I went out and sat in the barn.

"I hate her," I said to Tillie, who turned around to give me her sweet animal glance.

"When?" I asked Juniper that evening.

"In a week," she said.

"I don't want you to go."

She picked me up and sat me on her lap.

"I know. Nothing will make it any better, but you will be all right. I will think of things for you to do while I'm away."

"Work!" I said scornfully.

"Well, work does make the time go more quickly," she said. "And you enjoy it more than you think."

She did leave me a lot of work too. There was a long piece of writing to do in the script I tried to model on hers. There was some spinning. (I groaned when she mentioned this.) There was Tillie to feed and exercise. There was the poem about storms and clouds that I was learning to sing to the harp.

"You're not taking *Tillie?*" I asked disbelievingly. Actually, it would be very comforting to have Tillie as company.

"No. So you must take good care of her, and of the cats, and Daisy and the chickens."

I had to practice the harp, make cheese, put out food for Cormac, draw and carry the water I needed each day, prepare my meals.

"You will be able to tell me about it all when I come back."

"You will come back?"

"Wise Child!"

"Promise!"

"I promise. As much as anyone can promise it."

"You mean you might die?"

"I might. But I won't."

She said good-bye to me the night before she went.

"I will be leaving very early in the morning." She seemed to make no preparations, none of the elaborate packing of

food and possessions I remembered from Finbar's depar-
tures. I had felt sure that I would wake to hear her go, but
I slept so soundly under my bear's coat that it was broad
daylight when I awoke. I jumped up at once, and wrapping
the black fur around me, I ran downstairs in my bare feet.
Already a fire was burning in the grate and Ruby was purr-
ing in front of it. My breakfast was laid out on the table,
with a tiny pink winter flower in the middle of my plate. It
was very consoling, as real as a kiss.

I thought how easy it was to be alone now, when the
winter sun shone in the sky like a primrose and the sky was
a clear blue. I was scared of nightfall. But I would not let
myself think of that.

I milked Daisy, who was lowing angrily, fed Tillie, ate
my porridge, and washed dish and pan in the careful way
Juniper had taught me. I swept the floor, built up the fire,
and settled to my writing. I felt very busy, very grown-up;
I was enjoying myself more than I knew.

When the early winter twilight came, I bolted the doors—
something we never did when Juniper was at home—and
sitting on a chair near the fire, I tried to tune the harp and
eventually played it. Ruby pushed at my legs as if she too
missed Juniper.

Going upstairs to bed was scary. The shadow on the stairs
up to the attic wavered in the candlelight like a thin, thin
man, but I looked away, fled into Juniper's bedroom and
into my nest, pulling off my smock and blowing out the
candle in two quick movements. I felt safer in the dark
somehow. I wanted so much to go to sleep and not wake up
until morning, and to my pleasure and surprise I did just
that. I had survived so far. One day.

The second day was rather slower than the first. The

feeling of my cleverness at managing everything was giving
way to the sinking feeling of being all alone. At midday I
saddled Tillie and went down to the village. The young
children were at school, and my aunt was, unusually, alone
at home, apart from the baby, Nicol.

"Where's Juniper?" she asked innocently. I did not want
her to know that Juniper had left me—village people never
left their children all alone.

"She sent me down on an errand," I lied loyally.

"She is kind to you?" my aunt asked.

"Mmm . . ." I said, embarrassed.

"She must be feeding you well. You've grown."

"She does." I didn't want to discuss Juniper, just be with
a grownup for a bit. She gave me a cake, and when I had
finished it, put the baby in my arms so he would stop
crying, which he did. She talked about my cousins, but I
could feel her underlying curiosity.

"What's Juniper's house like, then?" I began to realize
that Colman said little, if anything, of his visits to the
white house.

"You should come and see it one day," I said, but I knew
she wouldn't.

I could not stay long. I did not want to risk being out in
the dark, and I had to feed the animals and shut them up.
The fire had gone out when I got home, and I could not be
bothered to relight it. I ate my supper and went straight to
bed, wanting the morning to come quickly. Perhaps because of this I woke up in the dark, hearing a purposeful
creaking on the stairs. The door softly opened, and there
was the quick patter of feet and a thump as Ruby landed
heavily on my chest.

"Oh, Ruby!" Even with the cat's presence I was lonely,

and the night seemed to stretch on forever. Dawn was gloomy and ominous, an angry red like a sore eye. I was sick of being brave and sensible; I just wanted not to be alone.

I felt tired and sad when I got up, but I forced myself to wash and dress, to sweep the ashes from the fire and relight it, to put the porridge on the fire while I went to milk Daisy. Looking after the animals helped a lot—I even got out Tillie's brush and groomed her carefully, knowing how much she liked it. I made the same hissing noise Juniper always made as she worked on Tillie, and the donkey turned around and looked as if she thought I might be Juniper.

So that it seemed like a reward when I went back into the house and there, coming through the doorway, was Colman.

"Mum said you came yesterday. I thought you might need something." He was his usual small, cool self.

I told him about Juniper being away, though without telling him how lonely I felt, nor how delighted I was to see him.

"What about school?" I asked him.

"I played truant."

I looked at him with admiration. Colman did not like breaking rules much—for him it took courage. I didn't mention it, of course, but started at once to cook, knowing that he would be as hungry as ever.

We sat together on a cushion in front of the fire, eating eggs and bacon and toast and a hot drink Juniper had taught me to make out of dandelions. As before, I watched his pale face fill out with warmth and food. When he had eaten, he was full of questions.

"What about the cellar? And the jewels?"

As it happened, I *had* discovered the whereabouts of the cellar. Juniper and I had been cleaning a few days beforehand—Juniper had moved a table, shifted the wall hanging behind it, and said, "Look, Wise Child, the door goes to some caves under the cliff."

"May we go down there?" I asked, shining eyed.

"One day, when you're a bit bigger and we're not so busy."

The door had heavy bolts, which puzzled me a bit—why should anyone want to get *into* the house from the cellar? When the tapestry swung back again, all was hidden, however.

"I know where the cellar is," I couldn't resist telling Colman. "Only we can't go there." I could feel an ineffably smug expression settle over my face.

"Don't believe you," Colman said jeeringly. "You're just making it up."

We quarreled about the cellar for a quarter of an hour, Colman insisting that I did not know where it was, and I swearing that I did. In the end I thought that there would be no harm in *showing* him the door.

"Now's our chance."

"It's locked."

Before I could stop him, Colman had pulled back the tapestry and started unfastening the bolts, though he had to stand on a chair to reach the top one. He turned the handle, and the door began to creak open.

"No, it isn't," he said.

"Juniper wouldn't like it."

"She wouldn't know. We'd be back before she returns."

"Juniper knows everything."

"If she really didn't want you to go down there, she'd keep it locked."

"Juniper doesn't think like that." All the same, I reasoned, I had gone into the attic without asking her, and she hadn't minded at all. And she had shown me where the cellar door was without any hesitation. I didn't know what to think.

"It's dark," I said.

"We could take candles."

"Or the lantern," I said, being helpful. I didn't want Colman to think I was scared, which I was.

"Think of jewels," he said, his eyes big. "Great handfuls of rubies and emeralds!" Colman and I were both fascinated by the idea of heaps of jewels. He had led and I had followed from as far back as I could remember. I forgot Juniper and my fears of what lay beyond the cellar door.

"We could just take a look."

Together we stood before the door while he swung it back. There was a flight of steps—neat, clean, like everything that belonged to Juniper—that went down into the darkness. In five minutes I had fetched the lantern and lit it. I had put another candle end in my pocket, and the two of us had begun the long descent.

part of the tunnel, and first Colman, then I, pulled ourselves up.

It was a beautiful sight. The light was quite dim, and came from a small crack in the rock about a hundred feet above us. We were on a shelf of rock, and falling in front of us was a solid sheet of water. It fell many feet below into a natural basin of stone, and from there flowed out, I supposed, through underground channels into the river we both knew well. On each side of it were great hanging ferns, which filled the whole cavern with a green, mysterious light, rather as if we were under the sea.

"Oh," said Colman, his face alight with the wonder of it. "Isn't it lovely?"

At first it seemed, as before, that there was no way forward. But this time it was I who discovered foot- and handholds that moved downward from our ledge; and it was I, so recently freed from fear of height and of water, who went first this time, encouraging Colman (who hated heights himself), even finding places for his feet.

"Easy, wasn't it?" he said nonchalantly when we got to the bottom.

We were puzzled for a moment, because such path as there was seemed to lead right into the curtain of water. We both guessed what that meant and, holding hands, we dashed through the side of the waterfall. Soon we were safe behind it, gasping from the cold water, on a rocky path in a gray waterworld. Colman said something but I could not hear him, the water made so much noise. Both of us, however, were in a mood of exaltation—just the two of us in this marvelous place. We hugged each other and laughed with pleasure.

This rocky path led to another ledge on the other side.

This time we had to edge our way out for about twenty feet along a ledge no wider than nine inches, uneasily aware of the tumbling water and the sharp rocks beneath us. I was glad of the day with Juniper when I had crossed the stream. Neither of us dared breathe as we made this part of the journey—both of us trembled slightly when the path widened and led downward toward a dark passage.

"We mustn't forget we've got to get back," I said in a fussy, grown-up way.

The path wound down and down for perhaps a mile. We passed through a series of caves into the biggest chamber I had ever seen—like a banqueting hall or a huge barn without any hay in it. Just holding the lantern aloft did not reveal the height of the roof, which I guessed was many feet above us. The diameter of the room appeared to be several hundred feet. As we walked around the perimeter of it, we noticed what looked like chairs carved in the rock—thrones really—and one enormous throne at one end. On the walls were sconces for candles.

The sheer size of it made us feel small and foolish. We felt even more foolish when we decided to leave the chamber and go on our way. We discovered that there were many tunnels out of the chamber, that all of them looked alike, and that we could not remember which one we had come in by.

"The throne was to the left of where we came in."

"No, it wasn't. We only noticed it after we had walked around."

"Don't let's go any farther. Let's try to find the way we came and go back."

Colman did not disagree.

We tried several of the tunnels one after the other, but none of them seemed to lead to the caverns, the tunnel, and the ledge. We tried listening hard for the sound of the waterfall, but it was too far away now to guide us.

"I'm hungry," I said.

"Shut up!"

"Shut up yourself!"

We might have pursued this quarrel, but I had begun to notice that there were paintings on the walls. Lifting up the lantern, I saw a picture of a sort of table with what looked like a kid on it and a man in a mask standing over it with a knife, cutting its throat. I had often seen men in the village kill the spring lambs like that.

"Look at this!" I exclaimed.

The next picture showed a girl, a bit older than me, wearing a white dress and carrying flowers. She was walking in a procession. Fascinated by this, I moved on to the next painting. She was lying on the table just like the kid, and the man with the knife was approaching her.

"Oh!" I said, frightened. I could not resist looking at the next painting. This one was quite different. It showed an enormous, terrifying devil, sitting in a room very like the room we were in. The same girl was held in his mighty hand, and he appeared to be eating her.

I suppose because I was so horrified by this picture, I began to back away from the wall toward the center of the room. I do not have a very clear idea of what happened next, only the recollection of the ground being no longer under my feet, and the appalling feeling of falling through space. I gave a shrill scream.

10

Rescue

THE TERROR of falling through the air was swiftly followed by pain as I hit the stone floor with a shattering bump. I struck my head against the wall as I fell, and from what Colman said later I must have fainted for a few moments. As I fell the lantern shot out of my hand and rolled away, leaving both of us in total darkness. When I came around, I was puzzled. I was not in my bed at home, because I was cold and damp. There was a bad pain in my leg that made me groan.

"Wise Child!" Colman was saying frantically from above. "Are you all right?" My leg hurt so much that I wished I could faint again, but I knew that I must speak to Colman.

"My leg hurts terribly," I said. I could not remember quite how we had gotten into such a dreadful predicament nor think clearly about what we had better do. I could think only of pain. For the next hour or two I drifted in and out of consciousness, sometimes in a sort of bad dream in which some huge animal was sitting on my leg, sometimes coming back to the reality in which I was lying at the bottom of this hole—what was it? an empty well?—and Colman was desperately trying to carry on a conversation with me. The cold bit into me until my teeth chattered.

When strange sounds started echoing through the cavern (to Colman's terror) and when, eventually, a yellow light shone through one of the many entrances to the big chamber, I did not know it. I only returned to consciousness when I heard a conversation going on overhead, Juniper's clear, cheerful voice comforting Colman's scared and tearful one. The next thing I knew, Juniper and Colman were kneeling beside me, spreading her cloak on the cold stone floor and easing it, oh so gently, underneath me. Even that was terribly painful, but I was soon warmed by its touch. By the light of her lantern I could see that I was in a round chamber, like a room with no roof to it, a big hole dug in the floor of the big room above. A short flight of stairs passed downward from the upper room on the other side of the circle from me. Between me and the stairs was a sort of stone table with runnels down the side of it and a sort of trough around the bottom.

Juniper had taken a vial from the basket she carried, and she held it to my lips.

"This will ease the pain, Wise Child," she said. For once I did not argue or make a fuss but drank it gratefully, longing for the pain to go. I lay back and groaned again.

"Now," she said briskly, "if I show you how to get back to the waterfall, Colman, do you think you could get back to the house by yourself?"

"Of course!" said Colman sturdily, though he must have been scared.

"You're not going to leave me?" I wailed.

"Just for a short while. I'll come straight back. Colman, I want you to run straight to Cormac's house—do you know where that is?—tell him what has happened and ask him to come and bring his ladder and some cloth we could use to attach Wise Child to it. We shall have to carry her back on it."

"Down that tunnel where you crawl?" Colman asked, horrified.

"No, there's an easier way than that. But it's secret, and neither of you must tell anybody, about that or anything else about the caves."

I was very frightened during the time when both Juniper and Colman left me. Juniper had lit a candle from the lantern and placed it beside me, but it flickered eerily and I hated the high stone walls of my prison. Faces swam in and out of my vision. One of them, a woman's face with long red curls floating about it, troubled me particularly because of its expression of contempt. Suddenly I remembered a piece of advice Juniper had given me one night when I was afraid of the dark in the barn as I milked Daisy.

"Make a ring round yourself. Ask Jesus to make it if you like. Then feel that you are quite safe within that ring— that that is where you are protected." It had helped in the barn, and it helped now as the warmth of Juniper's good warm cloak also helped. All the same I was very glad to hear her voice when she returned. She came down the steps, squatted on a corner of the cloak, and lifted my head gently onto her lap.

"It's all my fault," I said, beginning to cry.

"And Colman said it was his fault," she said, laughing.

Juniper always managed to find something funny in even the most desperate situations.

"I'm sorry the pain's so bad," she said.

"Already it's not quite so awful," I replied.

We were silent for a few moments. Juniper's medicine had pulled me out of the strange floating feeling I had had before. Now I knew where I was all the time.

"What is this place?" I asked her.

"We'll talk about it when we get home. Would it help if I told you a story?"

"Yes," I said, mainly to please her. I could not imagine any story that would distract me from this horrible place and the pain in my leg.

"Very well, then," she said. "I will tell you about when I was a little girl." I had often begged her to tell me this story, but she had always refused, and now, when I was in too much pain to listen properly, she wanted to tell it. It turned out, however, that she was quite right. I was so fascinated by the story she told that some of the time at least I did forget my own troubles. Juniper had once been a little girl like me, only in Cornwall. She had been the daughter of a king but had been kidnapped to Brittany, stolen away from her mother and father. Eventually, with Euny's help, she had found her way home again, but her old life had changed and she had wanted to go and live with Euny and learn from her how to be a *doran*.

We were both silent for a little when Juniper finished her story. It was extraordinary how the vivid picture of Cornwall and Brittany she had told me had lifted the weight of the dark and the cold, as the drink she had given me had eased the pain. She, I felt, had temporarily lost herself in that earlier world and had to be given time to return. She did so quite quickly.

"Cormac and Colman should be here soon," she said with her usual cheery confidence. "I must give you something to make you go to sleep, Wise Child. Otherwise the pain of the journey will be bad." She felt in her basket again and produced another flask. This one had a black, earthy smell that struck my nostrils as soon as she removed the cork.

"Ugh!" I said, but I dutifully took a big swig of it though it made me shudder with horror.

"Good."

"I hate not being awake," I said.

"Trust me," she said, and of course I did.

After that I have only a very vague recollection of waking up once or twice with a bad twinge of pain when she and Cormac jerked the stretcher on the way home. At one point, to my surprise, we seemed to be out of doors, under a cloudy sky. Colman told me later that having left the cavern, they descended by flights of stairs and then by a sharp decline into a long tunnel that eventually wound its way out by trees and scrub to a place quite near the village. (There was a boulder placed against the entrance, which they had to push away.) He was surprised no one in the village had ever told him about it, and Juniper, unusually for her, swore him once again never to speak of it except to me.

By the time I was fully awake again, I was back in bed at home, the bonesetter had come, and he and Juniper were talking of grinding up comfrey root, mixing it with water, and making a case to protect my broken leg. Juniper looked very tired, as well she might. For several days I was in a lot of pain, too much to want to talk or to feel bored, but

gradually I began to feel better and to make Juniper spend
many hours telling me stories, or talking to me.

"Aren't you angry with me?" I asked Juniper once. "It
was very naughty of us to go into the cellar."

"It was wrong of me to leave it so that you could get into
it so easily," she said. "But angry? No, I'm not. People do
what they do when they do it. Being angry is usually a bit
beside the point. What matters now is getting your leg well
again so that I don't have to do all the work."

"Huh!" I said, but as I lay there with my leg stuck in its
case of comfrey, even weeding seemed like a delightful way
of passing the time.

"You're not like most grownups, are you?"

"Not much!" said Juniper cheerfully.

"What goes on down there? Down in the caves? I saw
something really horrible on the wall there. The Devil
was . . . That was why I fell down the hole—I was so
frightened."

"They have a long history, those caves," Juniper began.
"At one time, you know, people thought that if they didn't
keep on the right side of the gods—if they didn't sacrifice
animals and maybe people—there would be no harvest, no
young animals, no nuts or berries, and everyone would
starve. So they had rituals, as *dorans* do, only theirs were to
keep the gods pleased with them and on their side. They ate
the sacrifice and it was like eating God."

"You only eat God in the Mass," I said.

Juniper didn't answer, though I felt she disagreed.

"Anyway, it was the Devil I saw up there on the wall,
and he was eating a person . . . a girl it was . . ."

"They were trying to keep on the right side of the Devil,

too. Or to get him on their side. There are people, you know, who are not trying to live in the rhythm, but just to control other people, to make them feel guilty or do what they want."

"Fillan Priest often makes me feel guilty."

"He does, and I wish he didn't, but it's not him I mean. There are much worse people than Fillan, who control other people with special sorts of spells."

"Sorcerers, you mean?"

"That sort of person. It doesn't matter what you call them. Once you start controlling other people, whatever your motive, you become a sort of sorcerer. Those people are not on the side of life, Wise Child, but they are powerful."

It flickered uncomfortably in my mind that Maeve was a sorcerer kind of person, but I pushed the unwelcome thought away. "Is that why you are here? So that the sorcerers can't come back?"

"Who knows? They won't if I can stop them."

I lay on the cushions in front of the fire and thought this one out. I had another question for Juniper.

"Juniper? Are you terribly rich? My cousins said you had a whole treasure chamber full of precious stones in the caves under the house."

Juniper hesitated. "Wise Child, there are children in the village starving at this very moment. Do you think I would keep rooms full of precious stones if I could feed them?"

I had never thought of that.

"It would have been lovely," I said wistfully, "to pick up great handfuls of diamonds and rubies and pearls and let them run through my fingers."

Juniper laughed.

"There are places in the East like that. The jewel chambers of emperors and kings. Perhaps one day we will travel and see them together."

I lay contentedly on my pillows, dreaming of sparkling stones and milky pearls.

11

Secrets

BY THE TIME I was up and about again, the tiny,
painted faces of the snowdrops were showing in the
garden. I noticed too that the light was changing day
by day, that the buds were showing on the bushes, and that
in the evenings the blackbird was singing his special just-
before-spring song. Juniper was cutting a dress for me from
a bolt of shimmering green material—the most delicate pale
green, like the color of beech leaves in early spring when they
are only half out and surround the tree in a green cloud.

"For me? In that marvelous silk? Where would I wear
it?"

"At Beltane."

"At Beltane?"

All I knew about Beltane was that it was the time when
people took their sheep and cattle up to the shielings—the
summer pastures. Yes, and that it was the time they lit fires
on all the hills—to Fillan's disapproval.

"It is the great feast of the spring, of course—the time of

joy and thanksgiving and pleasure. It is one of the times when we meet."

"We?"

"Those who live . . . in the rhythm. Who watch the seasons. Who die with the winter and rise with the spring." (She seemed to be talking more to herself than to me.)

"There's a feast?"

"Yes."

"Where?"

"A long way from here. Several days' journey."

"What will I have to do at it?"

"Say some words, which I will teach you beforehand. Walk in procession to the ceremonies."

She was draping the material around my shoulders as she talked; I had never touched material so fine and delicious.

"You will have a green velvet mantle and a tiny crown. You will walk barefoot."

"Will there be other children there?"

"Yes."

"When will we go?"

"I will tell you near the time. One thing. Don't tell anybody. Not even Colman."

IT WAS HARD keeping secrets from Colman, especially as I wanted to tell him about my new dress. I was struggling with my promise to Juniper one morning when he and I were sitting up in the hayloft of the barn, snuggled under the hay for warmth, though there wasn't very much hay left now.

"Morag wants you to go and see her at home on Sunday after Mass."

"Why?"

"I don't know. She doesn't want you to tell Juniper."

I was puzzled. What could Aunt Morag have to tell me that Juniper mustn't know about?

"Fillan preached against Juniper again on Sunday. He didn't use her name, but everybody knew it was her he meant."

I had not been in church the previous Sunday because of a cold.

"What's he got against Juniper? She does no one any harm. She's kinder to people than he is."

"She's not a Christian, is she? He thinks that's wicked."

I felt torn. I knew that you were supposed to be a Christian, and I didn't want to be classed as a wicked person, but I knew Juniper wasn't wicked. She took care of me better than anyone had in my whole life. Before, behind the long words and the tantrums and the cocksureness, I had been lost and lonely and afraid. Juniper had found me, had placed me on her warm lap, had become someone I trusted more than I trusted myself.

"He's silly."

"I think he'd hurt Juniper if he could."

This started such a dark, fearful feeling inside me that I pushed it away and refused to think about it.

"Tell your mother I'll come," I said.

I did not tell Juniper that Aunt Morag wanted to see me—only that I wanted to spend Sunday with my cousins. Her generosity almost made me tell her on the spot.

"Why not take Tillie?" she said. "You'll get too tired if you walk it."

When Sunday came, it was a day of blue sky and brilliant frost. Every puddle was iced, and tiny frozen water drops

"Poor little Margit. So it's all work, is it?"

"No. There are stories, and songs, and . . ." I started to flounder. Life with Juniper *was* hard work, but not in the horrid way Maeve meant.

"Well, at least you look well-fed." Her words brought back an old feeling that I was a disappointment to her, perhaps because my looks took after Finbar and not after her at all.

"I thought it was time you and I had a talk. I want you to think about coming to live with me." Even Maeve noticed how I shrank this time.

"I know you think I deserted you, and that was hard for you. But just look at me. Do I look like a woman who could stay at home with nothing to do but look after a baby? And Finbar away at sea all the time? Not that he wasn't handsome—the best man for miles around—but that was no good to me if he wasn't actually ever there."

For a moment I saw it all through Maeve's eyes; although I shrugged my shoulders away from her arm, I continued to walk beside her. Even her voice was fascinating—low and expressive, though fiercely proud.

"You are a big girl now, and we could have fun together, you and I. You wouldn't have to do the housework if you lived with me, nor do any lessons that bored you. I could give you whatever you wanted—clothes, jewels, toys, ponies. You would love my house. It is big—it is filled with beautiful things—and you would have a room next door to mine, hung with tapestries and full of books. Lovely food to eat, too—all the sweets and cream you like. We are not meant for this dung heap"—she indicated the village—"you and I. I will travel with you—you can learn languages and how to dress beautifully so that one day young men will adore you as they adore me."

I do not know how long she talked, nor whether I have remembered her words accurately. I was under her spell, and what I was aware of was not so much her words as the radiant picture she painted of the life that might be. While she described it I wanted it passionately—it was like a terrible thirst inside me. I think what broke the spell was that Colman had come out of the cottage and was standing with his feet through the rungs of the gate, watchful, alert, concentrating his gaze on the two of us.

"There's Colman," I said.

"You don't have to make up your mind now," she said. "The offer is there for you. My house is only about a day's journey from here. In the meantime, I have a present for you." She reached under her cloak and handed me a stone. It was a pretty stone, I could see that, and I took it quickly from her, put it in my pocket, and ran away from her toward the house. As I drew near, Colman got down from the gate and silently opened it, and I ran through it and into the house. I snatched up my cloak, went out from the front door with Tillie's saddle over my arm, strapped on the saddle, and rode away without looking back.

JUNIPER WAS NOT at home when I got back—she often went to see Cormac on Sunday afternoons. Like a sick dog I headed for my nest and pulled the bear's coat over me. I think I heard her voice calling me, but time seemed to pass, and the next thing I knew she was sitting beside me on the bed.

"Wise Child. Look at me!" She burrowed into the bear

rug, uncovered my head, and turned it toward her. I mumbled the one word "Maeve."

Suddenly she bent and picked me up in her arms, bear rug and all, and carried me down the stairs. In a sense all was as usual—the sweet-smelling fire, the two great cats, the clean hearth, broth cooking on the fire, the scent of herbs drying in the rafters and of rushes on the floor. Yet it was as if I was seeing it all through a distorting mirror—the chairs and cats and fire tiny, away at the end of a long thin hall, everything slightly misshapen, a sound like whispering—a whispering of words that could not be heard that made my hair rise on my head with horror. There was a strange whiteness or blueness in the room that drained it of color. I sat rigid, my eyes starting out of my head, not speaking.

Juniper stood looking down at me, and I avoided her gaze, guilty and ashamed.

"Did she give you anything to drink?" she wanted to know. I shook my head. "Or any sort of present?" I hesitated, but before I could speak, Juniper took my silence for a negative.

"Good."

I felt relieved.

She moved to the table and began selecting herbs, which she pounded in the mortar and then strained into a cup. It made a golden-looking drink. Juniper, I noticed, no longer looked darkly glowing, but ugly and witchlike, her body bent, her hands grossly worn with work.

"Who are you?" I asked her as she handed me the golden drink.

"Your Juniper," she said. She went to the harp and started to play. To begin with I recognized the tune, but then something quite different began to happen to the music—it fell into great shapes that tumbled about the room. I sat and watched them, not touching the drink. However, some quality in the music reached me. It was as if a sudden sharp jerk took place inside me, and I was myself again. Juniper was Juniper, Ruby was Ruby, and Pearl was Pearl, and the room looked as pleasant and peaceful as it had always been. I passed a hand over my forehead.

"That was awful."

Juniper stopped playing and came and sat beside me. She was no longer ugly.

"You must try not to see Maeve."

"How can she do that to me?"

"Because you are not yet free of her. Part of you is still part of her. And because she is a very powerful woman. One day you will be free and she will not be able to hurt you anymore."

"She is very beautiful."

"Very."

"You wouldn't let me go to live with her, would you?"

"Only if you were quite sure you wanted to."

"She has a house only a day's journey away, you know. She offered me clothes and jewels and ponies and dogs and sweets and not having to do any boring things to go and live with her; she would make me into a beautiful lady whom young men adore."

"Tempting!" said Juniper with just the finest edge of scorn in her voice.

"I am her little girl."

This time Juniper did not answer. She sat still and silent in the way that was her particular gift.

"Colman saved me from her. He stood on the edge of the field by the gate and he watched. Otherwise I might have gone with her there and then."

There was another silence.

"I think I'll go to bed now," I said. I picked up the bearskin and moved toward the stairs, waiting for Juniper to say good night, but she did not do so. I was very tired and I wanted only to climb into my nest. As I took off my blue dress, I felt a weight in the pocket, and slipping in my hand, I drew out the shining stone. It was extraordinary. It was milky, but it had darts of orange fire in it. It was green and blue and lilac all at once, but each time you moved it only a little, there was a spurt of flame that reminded me of Maeve's flaming hair. I knew that if I showed Juniper, she would take it from me, and it was so pretty that I did not intend to give it up. I glanced around for a hiding place and remembered that beneath my bed I had a treasure box in which I had already hidden notes, beads, and a bird's egg. The fiery stone soon joined them.

12

I Run Away

I N THE DAYS that followed, something seemed to have changed between Juniper and me. The lessons I had loved began to seem less interesting, and the ones I didn't like—the ones that involved learning long, long passages by heart—began to seem unbearable. I had always learned quickly; now suddenly I became very slow and unwilling. It made me cross and disagreeable.

My problems with learning, however, were as nothing to my problems with the outdoor work or with preparing the herbs. Pearl could not get me out of bed in the mornings now—once or twice Juniper came herself, but in the end she just left me, and I would come down yawning long after breakfast was cleared away. (Which, in turn, made me cross and difficult for the rest of the morning.) I did not scald the cloths properly in the dairy, nor wash the plates clean. I left the smelly pots of herbs to burn on the fire, I spread the drying herbs so thickly that they got moldy, I burned a skirt in front of the fire and dropped a precious vase as I dusted it. I was not trying to be naughty or awkward—I was just absent-minded.

"You're in another place," Juniper said. All the things that had given me such delight in Juniper's house—the stories, the lessons, the songs, the lovely and plentiful food, her kindness to me, sitting on her lap, feeling that I was a child whom somebody wanted—all seemed not to matter anymore. I had no idea why. But I had known ever since I had left Maeve that I would have to go to her.

One morning when Juniper was away on a root-collecting expedition, and I was yawning over my Latin, I knew that I could not stay with Juniper any longer, that it was time to go to Maeve. I went upstairs, packed a few of my things in a basket, wrapped my warm cloak around me, and set off down the cliff path. It was a fine sunny morning, not too cold, and I skipped and ran, knowing that I must get to Maeve's house before nightfall. I skirted the village so that no one would see me, and I set off on the long walk northward. Since I had lived with Juniper, I had become used to long walks—filled with good food and wearing good boots, I found them no hardship.

I scarcely gave Juniper a second thought. In fact, I did not give anything much thought. It was as if my mind was cleared and emptied, concentrated on just one thing: the act of finding Maeve.

I remember very little about that journey, only that, tired and hungry, with twilight curdling over the landscape, I came to Salen and the walls of a great park. Away in the distance, on a rise, I could see a big house. Wearily following the wall of the park for what seemed miles, I came at last to some great iron gates with a cottage set in the wall

beside them. I knocked on the door. I could hear the sound
of a crying baby within, but it was a long time before a
woman answered the door, a woman with the marks of
poverty upon her. Her clothes were in rags, her teeth were
black, and her hair was unwashed and uncombed. I could
see, beyond her in a poor room with no fire, several small
children, equally bedraggled, sitting on the floor.

"Yes?" she said.

"I have come to see Maeve the Fair. She is expecting me."

"She didn't say she was expecting anyone." The woman
was plainly doubtful that I was telling the truth. "I can't
disturb her tonight."

"You must tell her I am here. Now," I said firmly. "Tell
her that her daughter has come to see her."

I could see a flicker of interest on the woman's face. "You
don't look a bit like her," she said.

"Nevertheless, I am her child. She told me to come."

The woman hesitated, then started to take off her apron,
though it revealed only an equally dirty dress underneath.

"I'll go up to the house and see," she said. Then, eyeing
me in a not particularly friendly way, "I suppose you'd
better come in and wait here."

It was not a room in which I enjoyed waiting. It was
bitterly cold; the baby, lying in a wooden box in the corner,
cried without stopping; there was a smell of excrement, of
decayed food, of dirty human bodies. The children could
not take their eyes off me, and the dirtiest of them, who had
a walleye, got to his feet with difficulty and toddled over to
look at me more closely, planting his sticky little hand on
my blue cloak. All the children were very thin and, I guessed,
even hungrier than my cousins.

Their mother was not gone long. Treating me with an obsequiousness she had not shown when she did not know who I was, she led me out of her house with a lantern and up the long path to the house. She insisted on accompanying me and led me to the big front door with steps leading up to it and a portico. She knocked on the door, which opened at once into an enormous hall with flags and a huge fire.

A mastiff rose to its feet from in front of the fire and lumbered curiously toward me, growling.

"Down, Fer!" said Maeve's voice imperiously, and a slim woman in a vivid orange dress rose from where she had been sitting before the fire with a young man.

"Well, Wise Child," she said with a world of satisfaction in her voice, "so you decided to come and see your old mother. A very sensible decision." She brushed my cheek with a kiss and rang a small handbell that summoned a frightened-looking girl of about my own age.

"Take my daughter to her room," she said coldly. "And find her some clean clothes. We will eat in half an hour."

13

Maeve's Daughter

THE GIRL showed me to my chamber, which was very large. There were long tapestries of hunting scenes that moved in the wind, as did the silk covers of the big bed. There was a fire in the grate—set against the wall, not in the middle as I was used to. The room was not so much pretty as grand, but what caught my eye at once was that a dress of yellow silk was laid out on the bed, with shoes to match it lying on the floor.

"Is it for me?" I asked. The girl nodded. She went into a room adjoining the chamber and brought a bowl of rosewater and a cloth. A little shyly under her gaze, I slipped off my smock and mantle and washed my face and hands. Since she obviously expected to wash my feet and legs, I let her do so.

She helped me into the yellow dress, with its matching stockings and shoes. Then she brushed my hair until it shone. Passing down the stairs, I looked in a mirror and scarcely recognized myself. I had never been so fine.

"Well!" said Maeve when she saw me. "So you *can* look pretty!"

I sat at her right hand at dinner, and she heaped my plate with delicious food—venison, fowl, many vegetables. I was very hungry after my long day in the open air, and though I had always eaten well at Juniper's house, I had never seen such food. In a long mirror on the wall I could see Maeve and myself, orange and yellow, sitting at the long table, with Aedan, the young man I had seen in the hall, on Maeve's left. He seemed nice, but I was now too tired to stay awake, and as soon as I had eaten, I began to yawn and long to close my eyes.

Maeve excused me and sent me to bed. The same girl, still apparently terrified, helped me off with the yellow dress and hung it in a closet, which I could see over her shoulder was full of other lovely dresses. She unfolded a thin sleeping gown and slipped it over my head. I could not wait to get between the sheets and close my eyes. The shifting of the fire disturbed me a little at first, then the cry of a night owl, then the wail of a cat. The shifting of the tapestries in the wind troubled me, and the bed felt big and strange. Then, tired as I was, I knew that I could not go to sleep, but for want of anything better to do I lay with my eyes closed.

I thought of Juniper and wondered what she was feeling tonight with my nest empty. I missed her, but pushed the thought away from me with the thought that tomorrow I would not have to get up early and milk the cow, would not have to sweep or wash or shred herbs or grind meal. Nor would I have to learn long, boring things by heart, nor translate impossible bits of Latin. I was sorry to be unkind to Juniper, but really it was her own fault.

Then I thought I heard the door open quietly, surreptitiously. I opened my eyes just a fraction. At first I could not see or hear anything, but then, between me and the fire, I made out the figure of Maeve in her orange dress. She stood quite still for several minutes looking at me, while I pretended to be asleep. Then she turned and softly went out again.

NEXT MORNING I slept late, and when I awoke I enjoyed all the luxury of life in Maeve's house. The girl brought me a delicious breakfast in bed.

"What is your name?" I asked her.

"Jeannie," she said, in a half whisper.

"Are you afraid of me?" I asked directly. I had not lived with Juniper all these months without picking up some of her habits.

Jeannie hung her head. "A bit," she said.

"Why? I'll not hurt you."

Jeannie did not reply, but I knew, as if she had spoken, that it was Maeve whom she feared.

"Don't be afraid. We'll have good times together. I'm glad you're my age."

She smiled a tiny smile, and I smiled back at her. Soon she was sitting on the bed beside me eating bread and honey. Later she helped me to get dressed, and I went downstairs. There was no sign of Maeve, nor of anyone else. I sat for a bit in front of the fire until I got bored, then I set off to explore some of the rooms, the mastiff following suspiciously at my heels. Beyond the hall was the big dining room we had sat in the previous night, and beyond that a big room with splendid carpets, mirrors, and embroidered chairs. When I went through the door at the end of that room, I found myself in a little dark passage with rooms opening off it.

One of the rooms was a tiny sitting room that had Maeve's rose smell about it. Next door to that was a room with shelves holding bottles, a table with knives and flasks upon it, and another shelf with books. At first I felt quite at home in this room, because there were bunches of herbs in it hanging up to dry, filling the air with a strong, wild smell. Looking closely at some of the herbs, I noticed with surprise that they were belladonna and wolfsbane. There was also a strange-looking root shaped like a man. I had never seen a mandrake root, but I guessed that that was what I was looking at.

On the floor were cages with rats and rabbits imprisoned in them, and some of them were dead. They were not a good sight, and I turned away in disgust. Then it seemed to me that the room had taken on a strange animal smell, only half hidden by the smell of the herbs, and I wanted to get away from it. Opening out of it was another room containing only a loom, about the size of Juniper's loom. Like Juniper's loom it was strung with many colors, and like hers it reminded me of something that I could not quite remember. Unlike hers, however, it left me with a troubled feeling, as if I was afraid, or anxious, or sad, and as if this was how the world was—dreadful and hopeless. Suddenly it came to me that their weaving changed how things were, making them joyful or bitter. I wandered back through the passage, the big room, the dining room, and so into the hall. Still there was nobody about. I looked out the window, but it was sleeting, so I could not go out.

It was nearly lunchtime before Maeve appeared, yawning. "Did you sleep well, my darling?" she inquired.

"Not very," I said. "There were a lot of noises."

"This afternoon will be too cold to ride," she said, "so we will go out in the wagon, you and I."

At first it was very exciting trundling along the road in the warm wagon. There were skins full of hot water under our feet, and the sleet streaking diagonally past the window seemed to make our space all the more cozy. It was fun to see fields and hedges and houses moving past.

"How poor the people are here!" I remarked at one point. People were plowing despite the sleet, although the ground seemed too wet to work, and there was a group of ragged children walking along the road staggering under an enormous tree trunk.

"They do nothing but complain!" Maeve said with contempt. Privately I thought rags and hunger were enough to make anyone complain.

Far out in the country we stopped at a pitiful cottage.

"Stay here," she ordered me. She was gone for about twenty minutes, and when she came out again her eyes flashed with anger.

"What's the matter?" I asked, a little frightened.

"I've just ordered them off my land. To teach the other tenants a lesson. Alpin had complained about the state of his roof."

"Oh, poor people!" I said. "Won't they have anywhere to live?"

"Quite the little Christian, aren't we?" she said. I was silent. If Maeve owned all this land, then the poverty of all these people might be her fault.

room. As before, she stood and looked at me while I pretended to be asleep. It was very odd.

NEXT MORNING I could not wait to get up and saddle the pony. I had decided to call him Bran. The stableboy helped me with the difficult parts of the harness and led the pony out to the mounting block. I scrambled onto Bran's back. He moved so gently under me, responded so swiftly to my least command, almost to the thoughts I had only just begun to have. We trotted along the avenue, then took off across the fields, cantering and even breaking into a gallop. It was a cold day, and the wind made his lovely mane fly backward. I felt as if he and I were one person.

"Oh, you darling!" I said to him.

The joy of riding made me glad to be alive in a way I had not been since I had left Juniper. I went running into the house ready to embrace Maeve, who was sitting before the fire studying her account books. Clumsily I tried to give her a kiss.

"Not now," she said.

"You are my mother," I said very loudly, angrily.

"Of course," she said, her voice cold and distant.

The fun of the morning was spoiled, and I sat down to eat the delicious lunch feeling miserable and angry. When I had finished eating, I went upstairs. I had wonderful dresses, lovely food to eat, a pony, books, and I still felt sad.

After a while Jeannie came in and I read to her. She herself could not read, and she thoroughly enjoyed the story about the princess who was so unkind that toads and snakes fell out of her mouth when she talked, and her sister who was so loving that pearls and roses fell out of *her* mouth.

"Were the pearls and roses actually *in* her mouth," Jeannie wanted to know, "and if so, how did they get out?" I had been wondering the same thing myself. Juniper would have known the answer.

It was nice at first not having to do any cleaning up or cooking or any other work, but after those first two days I began to pick up my dresses for myself and hang them up as Juniper had taught me.

"I'm supposed to do that," Jeannie said.

"I've got hands too," I said.

"But you're a lady," she said. So that was what it was. Ladies just sat or rode around. Other people did all the work. Juniper wasn't a lady, and I wasn't sure I wanted to be one.

After a week I finally admitted to myself that I was dreadfully bored. I missed the long conversations with Juniper, the jokes we made as we did Latin together or read English, the pleasure of sitting in front of the fire after a long day's work and hearing her tell a story; being out with her in all weathers; sitting on her lap. It was ungrateful of me, I knew. Maeve had bought the lovely dresses for me, the books and the pony. She even tried to talk to me. Also I was her little girl.

I went in search of Maeve. There was no sign of her in the hall or in the big rooms. I wandered along the passage and into the room where she kept her bottles and her herbs. In spite of myself I looked again at the animals in their cages. Then I did something that puzzles me to this day. For no reason that I could clearly explain I reached behind the jars and drew out what I already half expected to find—a doll made out of wax. The doll had black hair, and its face was blackened a little with soot. It wore a red dress and on its tiny hand it wore a ruby ring. Around its head, however, there was a piece of wire, twisted so tightly that it cut into the wax.

I had heard of people making wax images to make other people ill, and now I remembered that it was for finding such an image that Maeve had smacked me when I was a tiny girl—I had thought it was a dolly to play with. I did not know who that long-forgotten image had represented, but I knew that this one was of Juniper, my own beloved Juniper, and that Maeve was determined to hurt her, to make her ill, perhaps to make her die. With trembling hands I unfastened the wire, doing my best to reshape the wax.

Hiding the doll under my skirt, I went straight upstairs, wrapped my warm mantle around my dress, and ran down to the stable. I saw with relief that Maeve's horse was not in his stall, which must mean that she was out somewhere. Maeve, I had discovered, often made unexplained journeys into the countryside that took several hours.

There was really no hurry, but I fastened Bran's girths with unsteady hands—the buckles seemed much stiffer than usual. My problem would be how to get out of the park. If I went through the main gate, it seemed probable that the lodge keeper would inform Maeve as soon as possible, and the whole point of taking Bran was to get a good start before Maeve had me pursued. Around all the rest of the park was a high stone wall—too high for Bran and me to jump. Only in one place that I had seen was there a wooden gate. It was locked, I had noticed the previous day, but I thought that we might jump it.

Suddenly excited at the thought of the journey, I coaxed

Bran first into a trot and then into a canter. Away in the distance I could see the white gate, and I, who had never jumped a horse before, quaked inwardly. But then I felt Bran's marvelously sure body beneath me.

I leaned forward, whispering in his ear, "Go like the wind." All fear left me, and I could feel the pony gathering himself beneath me, timing himself perfectly for the lift and the leap that cleared the gate.

"Good boy!" I said. We now had to ride past the lodge gates, and I thought it better that the lodge keeper should not see us and wonder about me. Accordingly, about a hundred yards away I moved from the road, led Bran onto the grassy verge, and walked him slowly past the house. To my horror I saw that Maeve's horse was tethered at the gate, which meant, presumably, that Maeve was somewhere within. I slipped down from Bran's back and walked him past the house, terrified that Maeve might look out the window and see me in the road. But no shout came from the lodge keeper's house, and a little farther on I got back onto the pony's back and began to trot. With luck it would be another hour before Maeve knew that I had gone.

I hoped that by riding at night, even if I was pursued I might evade my pursuers. But this meant that I would need to hear them coming and take cover before they heard or saw me. I felt as if every nerve was awake, that my sight and hearing were sharper than usual, trained backward along the road that I had come. Bran seemed to enter into the spirit of the thing. He was frisky, though obedient, going as if he would never tire, joyful in his gait as if he asked nothing better than to take part in this adventure. He was the perfect companion.

After a while the moon came out. This troubled me rather, since I knew that I could be seen far away on the road. On the other hand it made traveling much easier. Perhaps, in any case, Maeve would not bother to pursue me. It seemed to me now that she had only wanted me to spite Juniper, as if I was another form of the wax doll, used to cause pain.

More important than any of these thoughts was Juniper herself. Had Maeve's malicious action hurt her in any way? I desperately needed to find out.

It was a long night. About halfway through it I felt sleepy and dozed off in the saddle, but although I longed to lie down, I knew that I must not stop. I talked out loud to Juniper to keep myself awake.

Once I thought I heard a horseman on the road. Not sure if I had been asleep and dreaming, I drew into the shadow of a wood. Yes, there was the distinct sound of hooves, far away in the distance. The horseman came nearer and nearer and finally drew level and passed me. He was on a big black horse, and I recognized him as one of Maeve's servants.

I waited until the sound of hooves died away in the distance, and I could not think what to do. Since his horse was faster than mine, I was unlikely to overtake him. He would not know until he got to the village that he had passed me, so it should be safe to follow him. Unless, of course, he guessed what had happened and turned back. But I had already once heard him before he heard me—I guessed that my child's ears were sharper of hearing than his grown-up ones—and what had happened once could happen again. All the same it made me rather scared. It would be awful to be caught and led back again to Maeve.

When I reached the place where I could see the village away in the distance, I knew that I would need to be careful. A dull gray light in the east suggested that it would not be long before dawn. My advantage was that I knew this countryside as my pursuer probably did not. He would stick to the road, whereas I could cut through fields and so find a back way to the village. The main problem, though, was that I would have to go through the village, and he would undoubtedly wait for me there, or on the road between there and Juniper's house. There would be no problem about my approaching the village without being seen, but once I was in the village street there would be no evading capture.

The answer, of course, was to find Colman. I approached my cousins' house across the fields and when there gave our special bird cry. It was very early morning, and I doubted any of my cousins would be up. I called once, twice, thrice, and to my delight I saw Colman's surprised face at the window. He was gone for a few moments while he put on his clothes, and then he came out to the gate.

"Wise Child!"

The sight of a familiar face made me feel terribly tired and near to tears, but I tried hard to pull myself together.

"I have to get back to Juniper and a man is chasing me," I said. "He is probably on the road between here and the white house."

Colman never let curiosity distract him from the point of things. He responded immediately to my distress.

"We could go by the passage in the cliff," he said. "I know where it is."

"Could we push away the stone by ourselves?"

"I'm not sure. We could try."

"What about the pony?"

"Leave him here in the field. If the man finds him, we'll pretend we never saw you, we don't know how he got here. Well, the others *haven't* seen you and don't know how he got there. Truth always helps."

"How will I cross the village street?"

"I can go first and tell you when it's safe."

Colman's signal showed me that the man was nowhere to be seen—he must be farther along the road. I crossed the road safely, and we soon got to the big boulder.

"I've just thought," I said. "Juniper locks that door from inside, and she might not hear me banging."

"I know," he said. "I will have to go up the cliff the usual way while you go through the passage. Then I can tell Juniper to expect you."

"I'll get lost," I said in panic.

"No, you won't. If you keep straight along the passage, you will get to the waterfall, and you know the way from there."

By now the two of us were tugging at the boulder.

"I've thought of something else," I said. "I haven't got a candle."

"No? Bother. You can't creep around there in the dark. You'll have to wait just inside until we come to get you."

"Couldn't I wait outside?"

"Not a good idea. He might come in search of you."

Once we got inside, it wasn't so bad. There was a dry pebbly floor, and even, once Colman had pushed the boulder back, a hint of light coming from somewhere. Not the pitch blackness I had feared.

It was Colman an hour or two later who came and rescued

me from inside the cavern, holding Juniper's lantern aloft.

"Where's Juniper?"

"She's not been well."

"Did you see the man?"

"Yes, on a black horse. Waiting near the cliff."

This struck a chill into my heart, and we walked in silence. I thought what an odd return this was—by this inner pathway right into the very heart of Juniper's house.

"Is Juniper . . . does she seem angry with me at all?"

"She just said, 'Is she all right?' and I said you were and would be home soon. She was lying in bed."

We reached the ledge and the waterfall, and began to crawl along the interminable tunnel. Then there were the steps and the handrail and the plastered wall. Soon I was running up the stairs to Juniper's room. It was darkened, and I could only just see Juniper lying in bed.

"Juniper!"

"Wise Child!" She raised her head from the pillow and gave me a look of such love that I knew everything was going to be all right.

"What's the matter with you?"

"I have had the most dreadful headache. It's a bit better today, but the pain has been very bad."

"I think I know why," I said, and I told her about Maeve's waxen doll.

"Oh, was *that* it?" said Juniper with a touch of scorn. "Well, that makes me feel better," and she raised herself with a groan into a sitting position.

"I thought you might be very angry with me," I said humbly. "I ran away because I was sick of work and lessons and I wanted to live like a lady and not have to do anything."

"Was it fun?" asked Juniper with interest, as if she rather hoped it might have been.

"No, dreadfully boring. I missed *Latin* of all things, and all the other things that happen here. I never realized it was so much fun."

"It isn't always," said Juniper.

"No, but that matters less than I thought. What matters is being with you."

Juniper smiled.

"I'll remind you of that one day when we're out in the bog in the rain. No, but I know what you mean, and I am very touched. I am also absolutely delighted you have come back. I may work you too hard, but I love you, Wise Child."

"I know," I said. "That's why I've come home."

14

The Language

JUNIPER RECOVERED quite quickly once she had discovered the reason for the terrible pain in her head. She and I looked at the wax doll together.

"I never understand," Juniper said wonderingly, "how people can hate one another so much."

"Why does Maeve hate *you* so much?" I asked curiously.

"Many years ago Finbar and I loved each other. Maeve *persuaded* Finbar that he loved her better than he loved me, and he left me. But ever since then, even though she no longer wants Finbar herself, she has regarded me as an enemy. And in a way I am. I don't care for her sort of magic."

"She could use a doll again," I said. "Against you or me."

"No," said Juniper. "Not now we know. In the future we can protect ourselves with what I call 'clear water.' " Juniper made clear water with well water in which rowan leaves had been steeped. Each day we bathed ourselves in it, remembering to touch every part of our bodies.

My first thought, once I knew Juniper was all right, was for Bran. Colman told me later that the man on the black horse had caught the pony and taken him away—presumably once he realized that I was safely back with Juniper. To begin with I had nightmares that he might come to Juniper's house and snatch me away.

"He won't do that," Juniper said. "Maeve would have given him his instructions. A sorcerer like Maeve does not dare to trespass on the domain of a *doran* like me, just as I would not dare to trespass on her property, or at least I'd rather not. We both have more power when we are in our own places."

There was a question that I wanted to put to Juniper, only I did not really know how to put it into words.

"Maeve is wicked, isn't she?" I said at last. I was thinking not just of the wax doll but of the sad, ragged children I had seen stumbling under the weight of the tree trunk.

Juniper shrugged. "That's not a word I like to use," she replied. "She does not live in the rhythm, however—she uses her power for her own advantage, and that is always a pity because it does great harm."

"What I want to know is"—my voice trembled as I spoke—"if Maeve is wicked does that make me wicked?"

Juniper turned to me with a warm, loving smile. "Of course not," she said. "Perhaps you have some of Maeve's power within you, but you are going to use it for good. That is something that everyone has the choice to do."

"Was it wicked of me to run away to see Maeve?"

"I don't think it was, though it was a bit dangerous. You just needed to find something out for yourself."

"Did you mind when you found that I had gone?"

"I *missed* you," Juniper said carefully. "I love you, you see, and I love having you here. But you are free to leave whenever you wish."

I felt as if some cramped, frightened part of me had begun to expand inside me.

"I think I left partly to punish you. For making me work so hard," I said.

"Yes, I know," she said, and we both fell into silence.

"Aren't you angry with me then?" I asked at last, puzzled.

Juniper thought about it for a bit—I realized that she always thought before she spoke.

"No, I don't think I am," she said at last, and that seemed to be the end of that.

IF I HAD thought my running away would change anything in my life with Juniper, I was wrong. She still worked me just as hard, both at my lessons and at the household chores.

"You know, the more you can do, the more you need to be stretched," she said to me one morning as I was puzzling over some difficult mathematics.

"I hate being stretched," I said crossly.

The days were perceptibly longer now, if not perceptibly warmer. The cruel east winds of spring made our outings abroad miserable. Juniper never let weather interfere with her expeditions, and I was out with her and Tillie most afternoons, cold, grumbling, often wet. One of the memories I carry of Juniper is of her long hair blowing in the breeze, the rain running down her face.

It was on one such endless walk across the moor that Juniper began to teach me something of great importance.

Other people choose a tactful moment to say something that matters, if only to make sure of your concentration. Juniper never did that. She often chose a moment when I was tired, angry, busy, or hungry, and then told me something that cut right across my mood. So it was on that horrible afternoon when my hands were wet and blue with cold, as I carried an armful of wet heather. The wet had seeped into my boots, too, as it often did.

"I hate this," I muttered.

"What a marvelous cloud," said Juniper, looking up at the sky and not taking the slightest notice of my complaints. "Look. Like an old man with a beard." Then, without any beating about the bush, she went on, "By the way, there's a language you will have to learn."

"A language?"

"Well, it's *the* language, really. That's what the *dorans* call it. Eventually you will see why."

"Latin, Greek, French, English . . . there are too many languages," I said crossly.

"This is quite different. Truly. To start with you just learn the sounds. You never write it down, and you never learn grammar or vocabulary or anything like that."

"How do you know what it means, then?"

"By the effect it has. You will have to take my word for that. Just learn the words and see what happens. The other thing about it is, it's a secret language, and you must never reveal any of it save to other *dorans*."

Suddenly Juniper started speaking in this other language, and she said something that sounded like *Arrinyi glarm caroon*. Since I was obviously expected to repeat it, I did so sulkily. She repeated it again, and this time I got a little closer to her pronunciation. (These were not the actual words spoken; I cannot tell you those, of course.)

"What's it mean, then?"

"I told you, I can't tell you."

"Silly old language. I don't want to learn it. What if I don't become a *doran*?"

"You will forget it."

"How will I know whether to become *doran*?"

"Do you realize that now you ask me that question practically every week? Sometimes oftener. You will just have to see, like everyone else."

"Will I know better after Beltane?"

"Perhaps. I don't suppose so."

I felt very cross indeed now, tired of impossible words that I didn't understand, mysterious ceremonies, a vocation that might or might not be mine and that seemed to cut me off from everyone I knew except Juniper. I stood still, out there on the moor, where it was just starting to rain again and the sky was the dark, painful color of a bruised plum.

"I hate you," I said, and I stamped my foot. Juniper simply nodded and walked on.

I HAD MUCH more cause to hate in the days and weeks that followed. From that day Juniper started to teach me the language. It had to be learned by heart, sentence after sentence of it, each one as meaningless as the last. Time after time after time she made me go back to the beginning, to *Arrinyi glarm caroon*, and upon that foundation we built a whole edifice of lines that went on and on, apparently without end. In places it sounded like a list of things, in other places it seemed to have a kind of dramatic intensity. Some passages were, it seemed, sad, others joyful, even funny, judging by the expression on Juniper's face.

What was so odd was the way we worked at it. All of a sudden nearly all our other occupations were laid aside. We no longer read Latin or English, we no longer spent time over poetry or songs and stories, over mathematics or astronomy or music. Even the chores—cheese and butter making, cleaning, cooking, spinning, the work on the herbs—were cut to a minimum, or else Juniper made me recite strings of words as I chopped or stirred.

"Begin, Wise Child," she would say. *"Arrinyi glarm caroon . . ."* and wearily I would start the litany once more.

"If you would only tell me what it meant . . ." I would say tearfully, enraged at the sheer senselessness of it.

"I can't," she would say. "Or if I did it wouldn't mean anything to you. Everyone has to learn it this way."

"Have we nearly got to the end?" I rashly asked her once.

"Oh, nowhere near!" she said, laughing as if I had made a joke.

At first a whole evening, a whole morning, a whole afternoon, would be spent in the unutterably boring process of her speaking the words and me repeating them after her until I could remember them. It was cruelly baffling, sitting there, or standing—she preferred me to stand so that I did not get so sleepy—reciting words I did not understand hour after hour. Sometimes I felt as if the words were taking me over, sometimes I could not sleep at night because the words were running obsessively through my brain, and sometimes I burst into tears when Juniper made me go back to the beginning and recite it all once more.

"Be brave, Wise Child. It is hard, I know, but it will make sense one day, I promise you."

A thought struck me.

"Did you learn the language when you were young?"

"Yes."

"From Euny?"

"Yes. And she was much tougher about it than I am, I can tell you. She once made me do it all night. *And* begin work the next morning as if nothing had happened."

I could imagine Euny's determination.

"And were you glad later?"

"Of course. The trouble with it is there just isn't an easy way of learning it. Or I wouldn't make you suffer like this."

This was patently the truth. However cross I sometimes got with Juniper, I knew that she always told me the truth, in the way that some grownups don't, and that she always cared about me. It made up somewhat for the misery of my present life—rising very early in the morning, while it was still dark, racing through the chores, and then reciting until lunchtime. We would have a bowl of soup and a bit of cheese, and then recite most of the afternoon. Juniper then allowed me a walk or a game, we did the outside chores, had supper, and then I had to recite again until late at night.

"I don't think I can stand much more," I said to Juniper once. I had gotten past feeling angry or doubting the sense of what we were doing—it had *become* life to me, all by itself. For the past day or so I had had a sensation of something growing and swelling inside me, like a boil or an abscess ready to burst.

"You must keep going," said Juniper, and then I felt sure that I must, through my new and terrible tiredness, my busy dreams in which I sometimes now actually repeated words of the language, and through a state in which I seemed unable to eat or to sit still, to rest or to think, to read or to work.

One evening I was lying exhausted on the cushions by the fire, reciting as usual, and as usual struggling with sleep. Every time my eyes closed, Juniper would say urgently, "Stay awake, Wise Child!"

It was torture to stay awake—I wanted to go to sleep more than anything in the world. So tired was I that it seemed as if out of the corners of my eyes objects moved uncannily—a bunch of herbs hanging from a rafter, Pearl, the poker. The herbs seemed to be swinging in a nonexistent breeze, the cat to be gently floating in air, the poker to be wagging like a pendulum, but as soon as I turned, quickly, suspiciously, they were perfectly still. Then the sounds began, small rustling noises at first, as if I could hear mice in the walls. Sometimes it seemed more like a whisper, somebody speaking just too softly for me to hear what they said. A few minutes later worse started to happen; it was as if everything started to breathe— the floor, the chairs, the harp, the fire. I was plainly terrified. I could feel goose pimples coming out on my flesh, and the hair rising on my head.

"Everything's breathing," I said to Juniper. It came out as a sort of complaint. I could not tell her of my feelings, but I saw her eyes resting thoughtfully on me, as if calculating something.

"Good. Then try once more. *Arrinyi glarm caroon.*"

It did not occur to me not to obey. With infinite weariness, the words forced out of my mouth as if through thick porridge, I began the hateful recital all over again.

Almost at once something very strange started to happen. I realized this time that I was only conscious of the words for some of the time, and that there was now no longer any effort to remember. What was so peculiar was that this time I had the sensation that the words were uttering *me*, that sometimes I was the speaker and sometimes I was the hearer, that sometimes Wise Child disappeared altogether and sometimes I was more Wise Child than I had ever been before in my life. The words rolled on as mystifyingly as ever, and I was dimly aware that I was coming to the end of all that I had learned so far. I finished what I knew, and the words hung in the air for an instant, and then Juniper and I in unison began to recite lines that she had never taught me, and yet that were as familiar to me as my own self. These lines went on for what seemed to be another stanza and then stopped, whereupon something even more remarkable happened. Ruby looked up from her elegant pose on the hearth and remarked, in a voice both high and sonorous, "*Arrinyi glarm caroon . . .*"

"*Ruby . . .*" I said to Juniper in amazement, and I saw from her nod and smile that we had shared this moment. She came to me and kissed me.

"That's over, Wise Child. You can go to bed now and have a long night's sleep. Tomorrow you will try on the green dress, and on Thursday we will start our journey to attend Beltane."

I stumbled exhausted up the stairs, and Juniper helped

me off with my clothes and tucked me into my nest. She kissed me and sat beside me. I wanted, I *badly* wanted, to think about the strange thing that had happened to me, but I was drowning in the peaceful ocean of sleep.

"I was Not-Me," I mumbled to Juniper in one last effort to hold on to the experience.

"I know," she said. "Isn't it a strange feeling?"

15

The Feast of Beltane

APART FROM the night when I flew, I had never seen the mainland in my life until Juniper and I went to the Feast of Beltane. Setting off early in the morning, we walked through the silent village with Tillie clopping between us, our clothes and food in baskets on her back. We sailed across to the mainland in a *birlinn,* a galley with a bottle of holy water tied to her prow. Then we walked for miles through the hilly countryside until we left Dalriada behind. Exhausted from struggling across bogs and hillsides, we stayed with the Laird of Firkeld, introduced to me by Juniper as "the Green *doran.*"

Then, leaving faithful Tillie in the Laird's stable, we set off again on some fine fresh horses, including a little roan pony for me. We stayed at Tuile, in the island home of the Anchoress of Tuile, a Christian who also had the title of the Gray *doran.* Finally, at the head of the Great Glen, we turned west and then north. Three days after Juniper and I had left the island, we and the two other *dorans* arrived at an inn at the edge of the sea where the innkeeper and his wife greeted us as old friends.

"Tomorrow," Juniper said to me, "we arrive."

WE STAYED LATE in bed the next day, dawdled by the fire, talking and eating.

"Why don't we go?" I wondered, bored by the grown-up conversations.

"We go at dusk," said Juniper.

It seemed a very long, dull day to me. Several times I wandered out of doors, went down to the small clean beach where a number of boats were drawn up, threw stones into the water so that they would bounce off the surface, and looked across the long stretch of water to where I could dimly see islands in the distance. I had a feeling that puzzled me—of familiarity.

As the bright afternoon began to fade Juniper called to me; on the bed of our room at the inn she had laid out the beautiful green dress with its velvet cloak. There was hot water in a tub on the floor, and Juniper stood by the window weaving a garland of spring flowers. My heart gave a tiny leap inside me—of excitement, of fear, of a recognition that it was beyond me to explain.

With Juniper's help I bathed myself in the scented water. She dried me with a warm, rough towel, and then, very gently, slid the beautiful dress over my head. My skin shivered at the liquid touch of silk.

She fastened the broad girdle around my waist, combed my wet hair, and sat me down to wait while she too bathed herself. She put on a deep-red dress that seemed to bring flames up into her cheeks, and bound up her dark hair with a silver comb. I felt in awe of her, as if I didn't know her at all, she was so splendid. This did not seem to be the Juniper whom I knew day by day, at whose table I ate, and in whose rooms I slept. I lowered my eyes.

Soon my hair dried in the heat of the fire, and Juniper brushed and combed it, and then she took the garland and carefully placed it on my head.

"Come and look at yourself!"

I looked timidly. I was pale but unmistakably pretty. My hair, which had once looked so dreadful, rippled blackly in the mirror under its tiny flower crown. The dress was the finest I had ever seen, let alone worn. My eyes traveled in the mirror to Juniper, who smiled at me.

"Meet the Red *doran*," she said in one of her important undertones. "Thought you'd better know now." She bent and kissed me, fastening the velvet cloak around my shoulders with a clasp of green stones that looked like bright moss. We were ready to go.

The other members of the party were equally splendid— the Laird in a green mantle with an animal brooch at his shoulder and his shoes with silver buckles, the Anchoress in a gray gown the color of mist with her white hair beautifully dressed, the innkeeper also in mantle and brooch, with his wife wearing a golden torc and a snake armlet. The ship sailed gently across to the island, its white path and trees gradually becoming clearer in the evening light, the western sun giving it an extraordinary radiance. It grew dark and a little chilly, and I was glad of my warm cloak, which felt rich and splendid around my neck. We sailed on and on; my eyes were drawn to the phosphorescent glow of the waves. Juniper came to talk to me as I stood looking out at the prow of the ship.

"I will not be with you during the ceremony," Juniper said, "but don't be anxious. You will find that you know what to do. And whatever happens, and however strange it feels, have no fear. This is a night to be glad about."

I shivered a little at her words, though I didn't feel afraid exactly. I felt excited, as though anything might happen, as though the Wise Child who left the island next day might be a different Wise Child from the one who approached it.

There were many people at the little jetty where we got off the boat, all entirely silent. Juniper made her way through the crowd and disappeared. Everyone was moving slowly in the same direction. There were a number of young girls dressed like me, and there were older girls and boys dressed in white linen tunics and carrying torches, which they lit from a brazier behind the jetty.

Slowly the older girls and boys moved in twos up the winding path ahead of us, and the younger children, myself among them, followed behind. It was very dark now, and far ahead of us I could see the torches glimmering like fireflies. My sense of smell seemed unusually strong—I believed I could smell wild garlic and mint in the woods on each side of us, or maybe we were crushing it beneath our feet. As we walked, calm, unhurried, I began to hear the sound of a drum far away, solemn, slow, measured. Then came the husky, unearthly notes of a flute. It did not play a tune so much as ask a question, the question that this evening was putting to me. The path wound upward, became steep and tiring, then it wound down again. From far ahead of us, where the torches were bravely burning, came the sound of singing. The singers took up the question of the flute.

The path was descending sharply now, past a rushing waterfall on our right, around a curve that made the voices of the singers faint and the light of the torches disappear, though the thump of the drum seemed now to throb right through us. I noticed that we all walked in time to it.

As we rounded the curve, we found ourselves at the foot of an avenue of huge stones, and it was then, of course, that I knew where we were. I had come back to the place I had visited in my flying vision, the place that Juniper had said would be important for me. I felt very small and solemn in my fine clothes walking up that great avenue just as I had done before.

As before I came to the big outer circle of stones, only this time there were several hundred people grouped among the stones, and near the middle of the circle were the dying embers of a fire. The singing died away, and all of us stood there in silence. We were, it seemed to me, waiting for something. I could see people moving far away on the other side of the circle, and out of the dark emerged twelve figures in gold. Each wore a huge embroidered gold cloak, each wore a crown, and each wore a strangely wrought mask. I know now that they were masks, but my first thought was that these were gods, or supernatural figures. They were preternaturally tall, they appeared to glide over the ground, and the expressions on their faces! Their faces made my heart stand still and my knees turn to water. Their faces expressed joy, anger, laughter, grief. One mask was so cruelly ferocious that suddenly I wanted Juniper very badly, or else I wanted to get out of this strange place.

So frightened was I that I had a sensation as if I was falling through space, lost forever; but then, like a ledge presenting itself or a plant embedded on a rocky cliff that I could cling to, I heard the words that I knew as well as I knew myself.

"*Arrinyi glarm caroon . . .*" Automatically I joined in the familiar string of words, and my swift descent into nothingness was arrested. All of us were half saying, half chanting those extraordinary words whose meaning I did not understand.

I noticed that now the girls in white were moving among the people bearing chalices of silver, from which every person took a sip. I bent my head like the others and took my mouthful—a stony, mineral taste as if earth was mixed with the water. I wanted to spit it out, but I didn't dare.

Almost at once I became aware of something that I did not want to know. I knew that the king or lord of those gods in the center—the one with the oldest and wisest face—was going to summon me, and that I would not be able to move, that I would be rooted to the spot. The liquid I had drunk was running in my veins like fire—I began to sweat furiously, and to feel as if all of me had climbed up into my head into the tiny space behind my eyes.

I was walking toward that center space as if my legs knew something that I did not. In the middle of the stone circles was a flat stone, a rectangle, of which the narrow end was facing toward me. At the other end of this stone stood the oldest and wisest figure, who looked both stern and loving, fierce and gentle, innocent and wise. In his hand was a dagger.

I see, I thought. *He is going to kill me.* I was not angry, nor especially frightened anymore, but I was puzzled. Why should I be killed, and why should Juniper, whom I knew beyond a shadow of doubt to love me, allow it to happen to me? And where was Juniper?

I stood still at the end of the altar stone, trying to look straight and dignified, and as I did so the chanting died away. The words were nowhere near finished yet, so I wondered why they had stopped. Once again I felt that we were all waiting, only this time I slowly realized that they were waiting for me. I groped in the back of my mind for those familiar words, and I almost jumped when I heard my high voice, with a tiny tremor in it, actually beginning to recite them aloud. I continued alone for a verse or two and then, with the emphasis of thunder, the whole company came in with a sort of refrain. Once again, after a little, they stopped and I continued alone. Once again they joined in. It sounded like question and answer.

I realized that the crowd on the right of the altar had parted, and through the middle of it, both hesitant and yet as inevitably as I had moved myself, there walked a deer, exquisitely graceful, his great antlers held proudly, his face looking from side to side as if to see everyone who was there. The deer stood beside me, looking up into my face, and upon its antlers one of the god figures placed a tiny golden crown.

The singing continued, and to my surprise I began to know what The Language was about, not just the part we were singing now but the whole poem. It began with the praise and joy in all creation, copying the voice of the wind and the sea. It described sun and moon, stars and clouds, birth and death, winter and spring, the essence of fish, bird, animal, and man. It spoke in what seemed to be the language of each creature—I remembered Ruby joining in on the night I had finally mastered the poem. It spoke of well, spring, and stream, of the seed that comes from the loins of a male creature and of the embryo that grows in the womb of the female. It pictured the dry seed deep in the dark earth, feeling the rain and the warmth seeping down to it. It sang of the green shoot and of the tawny heads of harvest grain standing out in the field under the great moon. It described the chrysalis that turns into a golden butterfly, the eggs that break to let out the fluffy bird life within, the birth pangs of woman and of beast. It went on to speak of the dark ferocity of the creatures that pounce upon their prey and plunge their teeth into it—it spoke in the muffled voice of bear and wolf—it sang the song of the great hawks and eagles and owls until their wild faces seemed to be staring into mine, and I knew myself as wild as they. It sang the minor chords of pain and sickness, of injury and old age; for a few moments I felt I was an old woman with age heavy upon me.

Again the music stopped. There was silence for a long time. Then from far away on the mountain behind I could hear a boy's voice of intolerable purity, crystal pure as an echo. Why, why, why, his voice asked.

As if in answer, the deer moved forward, raised his head to stare straight at the chief of the gods, who in turn lifted his silver dagger. For a moment there was a line of ruby along the deer's beautiful neck, and then the creature dropped like a stone upon the turf, the bright light gradually leaving its big luminous eyes. I gasped, though not in horror. We were in a place beyond horror, where everything was understood in its true light. The deer had come in response to our singing, and had offered himself in response to our question. He was the answer to it.

There was another long moment of silence, and then the singing began again, very quietly, mournfully, yet hopefully. During this part I began to look more attentively at the gods in the circle, and with a little shock of recognition that actually made me jump, I became convinced that one of them was Juniper. Quite how I knew I am unsure. Certainly dark eyes glittered behind her mask—but others in that circle had dark eyes too. I just knew that it was she, as if I could smell her. I moved toward her and stood beside her. Her arm went around me, and at that moment I caught a glimpse of a crimson dress beneath her great golden cloak.

The great solemnity of the occasion began to give way to rapturous joy. A bonfire was lit, the sacrificial deer was cooked on it, and all of us partook of its sacred flesh. We ate many rich kinds of food, we drank wine, we danced. Juniper threw off her cloak and her mask and was again resplendent in her crimson dress.

We sailed back across the water as the sun was rising next morning, a delicate primrose of a sun in a pale-green sky. I leaned against Juniper, too tired for speech. When we got back to the inn, Juniper helped me undress, lifting my heavy arms, raising me to the lap of the bed, tucking me in, kissing me. I was asleep before she had drawn the curtains on the rising day.

16

Summertime

FTER Beltane I was full of questions. "When the man in the gold cloak summoned me to the stone and I spoke the words . . ." I began, "I wondered . . . does it mean that I am special?"

"How do you mean?" asked Juniper.

"There were lots of other children there, but he didn't summon them. Why did he summon *me*?"

"Somebody had to do it. Why not you?"

She was being very dense.

"But I felt as if I was the right person."

"Yes, you were the right person. Then. At other times other people are the right person for something."

"So it doesn't mean I'm special?"

"Everyone is special."

"It doesn't mean I am bound to become a *doran* or anything?"

Juniper didn't answer this time, but went on stirring the soup as if I hadn't spoken.

"I *want* to be special," I said obstinately at last.

"So does everyone else. So we have to take turns."

"But some people are more special than others, aren't they?"

Juniper suddenly got extremely irritated. "The *really* special ones are the ones who don't ever think about it," she said. I knew better than to pursue it any further.

AS THE WEEKS and months had gone by, the herbs that had once bored me had begun to interest me more and more. I loved the circular garden with the rows of spicy and sweet-smelling plants; I had fallen into Juniper's habit of idly picking a leaf and breathing the smell of lemon or aniseed, peppermint or sage. I knew now the common currency of our trade—the simple remedies of marigold and comfrey, peppermint and plum—the cures for cracked skin and wounds, for indigestion and constipation. Slowly, without too much encouragement from Juniper, I was beginning to learn about the drugs that relieve terrible pain—those dark, dusty, and dangerous drugs that grew against the stone wall of the garden and were for people desperately ill or for people who needed to sleep while smashed bones were repaired. I do not know why they interested me so much, but from the time Juniper first told me about them, I learned their names and their properties, watched carefully to see how they were harvested and kept, read about them with difficulty in Juniper's big books. My curiosity about them made me a better scholar.

Very gradually Juniper had fallen into the habit of taking me with her when she went to visit the sick people in the village. What had once seemed so repulsive had gradually

I felt a lurch of panic inside me.

"Mallie has done everything she can." (Mallie was the midwife, the layer out of the dead, the one who was the first on the scene when anyone in the village was ill or had an accident.) "You probably can't make him any worse."

I remembered my reading—the effect of the dangerous belladonna when mixed carefully with other soporific herbs. I might at least lessen Witolf's pain.

"I'll come," I said. I put a flask or two in a basket, and some herbs that might stanch bleeding, put on my cloak, and followed Ranald.

Witolf usually lived in a sort of shed at a farm on the outskirts of the village. After the accident, however, they had carried him into the farm kitchen, an enormous white-washed room with a vast fireplace. They had laid him in the gentle warmth of the hearth, surrounded, ironically it seems to me now, by the steaming kettles, the newly baked bread, and all the symbols of life.

Soon after Ranald and I reached the track leading to the farmhouse, I heard the most extraordinary sound—a cat, I thought it must be at first. When I realized what it was I stood stock-still, rigid with shock. What I could hear was a man screaming and screaming, a terrible, high sound that congealed in my ears. I did not want to go on. Ranald, however, took my elbow and led me forward, through the knot of farm workers. Something must be done for Witolf— stranger as he was—and I was the only person around to do it.

The terrible injury was hidden by a blanket—the wheel had sliced across his thigh—so all I saw at first was Witolf's pale, ghastly face, under his thatch of yellow hair, and his

glittering blue eyes searching desperately for help. The sight
of a little girl could not, I thought, give him much feeling
of hope. I knelt beside him and put my hand against his
cheek in the way I had often seen Juniper do to people.

"I know the pain is very bad," I said to him in English,
"but I am going to give you something to ease it. It won't
take long." And I gave him the draft.

I took his hand and sat beside him, and almost at once
the screaming sank to a sobbing, and the sobbing in turn
became an enormous sigh. I could feel his tormented body
relax.

"Will you look at that?" said Ranald.

"Holy St. Bride! . . . ." said the farmer's wife, crossing
herself.

Mallie, who had been stirring some mixture over the fire,
looked venomously at me.

Soon Witolf fell asleep, and one by one the ring of spec-
tators crept back to their jobs in the barn or in the fields.
The farmer's wife started making pastry, her enormous arms
covered with flour. While Witolf slept, I drew back the
blanket and covered the great wound with leaves, but I
knew that Witolf would die. It was nearly dark when he
suddenly opened his eyes—we were alone at the time—and
fixed me with his gaze. His speech was slurred, but I understood him.

"Priest . . . great wrong . . . don't want to be damned,"
he said.

When Fillan arrived, I slipped past him and out into the
storeroom that stood behind the kitchen. I heard their voices
rising and falling for a while. At one point I peeped through
the door, and Fillan, wearing his stole, was touching Witolf

with the holy oils. At another moment he was making the sign of the cross over him, his face grave, absorbed; the firelight behind him made a sort of aureole of his sandy hair—he looked like a saint in carving.

He passed me on the way out.

"What are you doing here?" he asked sternly.

"They sent for Juniper," I said, stammering. "She was away, so I came."

"She's bringing you up in her own path, is she? Spells and potions?"

I hung my head. "I am a Christian, sir."

"We shall see."

Witolf died, very quietly, within the hour, as if all the pain had gone from both his body and his mind. I was very tired as I climbed the cliff—I seemed to ache all over. But then there was the peace of the big room and the cats and Juniper's lap, and at last I could be a little girl again.

"You did well," said Juniper. "You were very brave."

Although it was a summer evening, it was cool, and Juniper had lit a small fire of driftwood.

"Wasn't it lucky I knew all about the herbs?"

"Very lucky."

"The herbs really work, don't they? Except that . . . I don't know . . . I thought the pain began to get better when I talked to him and held his hand. But then . . . he was still very frightened in a way that only Fillan could help him with. I don't like Fillan, but he made Witolf feel peaceful."

"It's not one thing that takes away pain. Sometimes it's herbs. Sometimes it is having someone take your hand. Sometimes it is telling somebody something wrong you have done and letting them take the weight of it away from you. Witolf needed both of you."

"But I'm only a child."

"You knew what you were doing and you cared about him. Those were the important things. Fillan cared, too, so that also helped."

"He was awfully nasty to me."

"Being a friend of mine can make life difficult. I am sorry about that."

"I want to be both a Christian and a *doran*."

"I see no problem in that. But Fillan may."

17

The Summoning Stone

ONCE AGAIN Juniper and I were gathering berries and nuts, peat and hay, to prepare ourselves for the winter.

"It will be a hard one this year," Juniper warned.

One bright September day she took me on a long journey high into the mountains. We walked for miles, sometimes climbing up steep parts on our hands and knees, stopping often to get our breath back and enjoy the view. We passed through a tiny green corrie that reminded me of Ossian and his mother, and exclaimed at the pleasure of seeing the deer there; they looked back at us, still, unafraid, curious.

"You know . . . that time at Beltane . . . I thought they were going to kill *me*," I said.

"Being ready for death—that is something one has to learn. Knowing that it doesn't matter. That's what makes it possible to live."

Finally we arrived, panting and tired, dripping with sweat, at a small wood of oak and hazel in a fold of the mountains, protected there from bitter winter winds. It was very quiet in the wood, and the bright light of the sky filtered through the leaves and made patterns on the forest floor. We moved, slowly, silently, as if the quiet of the place put a finger on our lips. We walked on for perhaps half a mile, then emerged into a small clearing. Juniper hesitated a moment there, as if uncertain of her bearings. The wood was very dense. Then with a swift movement she went over to a rock emerging from the ground and slipped behind it. I could scarcely believe my eyes. One minute she was there and the next gone.

"Round here," she called. I too slipped around the rock and found myself in a little alley cut between briers and brambles. We followed this thorny path for a while until it led us around to the right, and suddenly we were in another, much more private clearing. I heard it before I saw it—in the middle a small spring bubbled up beside a stone. On the stone stood a silver cup—it was placed exactly in the middle of a rune that had been carved there. Juniper and I stood one on each side of the spring. She filled the cup and passed it to me to drink, and when I had finished I did the same for her.

When we finished this tiny ceremony, we made our way home again.

"Why did we do that?" I asked curiously.

Juniper offered no reply.

I AM NOT SURE why, but the rune put me in mind of the stone with the fire in it that I had hidden under my bed at home after the meeting with Maeve at Aunt Morag's. I had not looked at it for months, but that night I took it out when I was in bed and Juniper was busy downstairs. The fire within it looked different at different times. This time it looked yellowy, though when you moved it, it gave sudden stabs of orange. It felt cold against my cheek. I thought of Maeve of the red Judas hair, and unexpectedly I longed for her. One day when I was bigger, I would go back to see her. But now I must live with Juniper and learn Latin.

"I'M GOING AWAY for a week quite soon," said Juniper.

"Good. I love going on journeys."

"By myself."

"Where are you going?"

"To visit a *doran* in one of the northern isles."

"Why can't I come, then?"

"Because we shall want to sit and talk for hours and you would be very bored. You know how you get."

I pouted. I hated it when Juniper wasn't there, and I didn't like her enjoying herself without me. Also a week was a very long time.

"See," she said, guessing my fears, "I am going to lend you this while I am away. It's a talisman with a special rune of protection and comfort written upon it." It was a flat piece of silver—you could see the marks where the hammer had shaped it. There were two holes in the top where a piece of leather went through it so that you could hang it up if you wanted.

"It's pretty," I said as its gleaming surface caught the light.

"Better than pretty," Juniper said.

She was especially nice to me in the days before she went—retelling my favorite stories, singing my favorite songs, cooking my favorite meals.

"You spoil me," I told her solemnly.

"Do you think I should stop?" she asked. And she winked at me.

"I am an impossible child. Everyone used to say so."

"*Used* to say so. Now I think you're rather nice."

I glowed with pleasure.

THAT NIGHT, as on other nights before it, I took out the hidden stone. It fascinated me that however often I looked at it, it was always different. Sometimes I even had the fancy that it was saying something to me, that if I listened harder I would know what it said. Sometimes I thought it was wrong of me not to tell Juniper about it, but then I would think, "It's only an old stone. Why would she mind?" But then if she wouldn't mind, why did I think it was better to hide it from her? It was very puzzling.

The day of Juniper's departure came. She took Tillie with her, and two big panniers. I was angry with her for going, and I kissed her aloofly and refused to show much interest in her journey, just to punish her. Before she had clattered out of the yard on Tillie's back, I had gone in and shut the door. I did not want her to see the tears I had already begun to shed, tears that I wept under the bearskin. She did not love me. Nobody who loved her little girl went away and left her. Presently my tears ceased. I wiped my face, dried my eyes, went downstairs, and ate all of the meal Juniper had thoughtfully prepared for my lunch, though we had only just eaten breakfast.

Then I took out my stone. It had never looked so beautiful. There were deep indigo, purple, and violet colors glinting in it. I raised it to my cheek. It seemed to be easier to hear what it said. I thought I caught the words "me" and "home" and "road." There was something rhythmical in its tiny voice, as if it was reciting a poem; I needed to know what the poem was. It was tantalizing to so nearly get the words of the little poem.

I took the stone out onto the steps, where Juniper and I had so often sat together.

> *"Wise Child . . . . to me,*
> *Over . . . . . hill . . . and sea.*
> *. . . . . , footsteps . . . .*
> *Take . . . road . . . . home."*

I put the stone down and wandered restlessly around the house and garden. I popped some fuchsia buds and some snapdragons, I crushed a leaf of lemon balm in my hand and smelled it, I went into the dairy and took a spoonful of delicious yellow cream and swallowed it. At this time of day I was usually reading and writing—around Juniper there was never a lot of time for daydreaming and meandering—but since Juniper was not here, I saw no reason not to give myself a holiday. However, as I soon discovered, it did make the time go awfully slowly.

A bit later I went back to the stone and picked it up again. It was now warm from lying in the sunlight, and as if this had infused it with energy, its tiny voice was louder and clearer than ever before.

> *"Wise Child, will you come to me,*
> *Over land and hill and sea.*
> *No longer let your footsteps roam—*
> *Take the road that leads you home."*

I am not sure that I ever heard separate words of it, just like that, but I heard enough to get the sense of the whole. I heard something else, too: that the voice was Maeve's.

I felt at once excited, pleased, and very afraid. Maeve, the beautiful Maeve, *did* love me and want me after all—she had missed me when I had gone. She must be at her great house on the mainland (over the sea, the poem said), where I should lead a life of joy and luxury—never have to muck out the cow's stall, churn butter, chop herbs, or learn long poems by heart. Maeve might not be very easy to live with, but she would find me a handsome husband—rich and famous too—and I would live happily ever after. Somehow I had managed to forget all about the horror of the wax doll.

But I did at least think of Juniper: Juniper, who did not think in terms of luxury and handsome husbands, but who lived as if everything in life—some evil-smelling ointment she was making, an old man with the dropsy, a deer, a bit of Latin poetry, the taste of the butter, the color of the mead, the feel of wind or rain or sun or tempest, the sound of thunder or the stab of lightning—was a joyful and wonderful treat, a source of amusement, of pleasure, of fascination. Juniper had a secret, though not the sort you can easily tell, and I wanted to be someone who shared that secret.

I wanted to learn, too, to lose myself in the pleasure of books, of stories and thoughts, to learn more about healing people, to know about astronomy and geometry, about people who had lived in history, to be able to talk in foreign tongues and to sing and play the harp. I also liked the way Juniper kissed me and comforted me, listened to me, understood what I was trying to say to her even when I got the words all wrong, never made me ashamed if she could help it. She had taken me in when, because of Maeve's neglect, I was homeless, she had fed me and clothed me, taught me and sung to me. How could I abandon her?

When I went to bed that night, I put the stone on the floor beside my bed and went to sleep feeling quite peaceful. Even if I *had* decided to join Maeve, there was no way in the world I could get to the mainland. I had no money, no boat, no horse, no map. But I woke an hour or two later with the moon streaming in at the window. I did not touch the stone, but it seemed to me that I could now hear it reciting its little rhyme quite clearly:

> *"Wise Child, will you come to me,*
> *Over land and hill . . ."*

I was terribly afraid. On an impulse I jumped out of bed, ran across the room to Juniper's bed, and hid myself under its covers. I pulled them over my head and could no longer hear the mocking little voice. Presently, when I pushed the blankets off my face, it had stopped.

The next day I decided that routine was the best cure for terror and the supernatural. I got up early, made porridge, fed Daisy and the chickens, turned some drying plants, swept the living room, did some reading, even learned some more English words. In the late afternoon I went for a walk and came back with some honeysuckle, which I put in a pitcher on the table. I prepared supper. All day I had not touched the stone nor gone near it, but after supper I knew that I could not postpone it any longer. As I picked it up from the floor it was caught in the rays of the westering sun, and for a moment it was colored bright vermilion.

I held it to my cheek as before, but to my surprise, yes, and dismay, the voice had sunk down again and I could not distinguish the words any longer even now that I knew what they were. I carried the stone downstairs with me and tried it several times over the next hour, but it was no good. I could not hear it. Had I displeased it in some way?

The next morning I tried it again, but it was still a faint burble of a voice. Remembering what had happened two days before, I left it outside on the steps in the sunshine for half an hour and tried again. To my joy the words were now much clearer, but to my astonishment they had changed.

> *"Wise Child, raven-headed girl,*
> *Best of daughters, Finbar's pearl,*
> *Ford the river, cross the sea,*
> *Come, my dear one, unto me."*

Once again I felt filled with intolerable longing for Maeve. "I'm coming, I'm coming," I told the stone, only to remember as I said it that there was no way I could get to the mainland, nor to Maeve's house. I wept, this time with the bitter disappointment of not being able to obey the stone. I began to talk to it as if it was a person.

"I *can't* go to Maeve," I told it, and I wrung my hands.

That day the chores were perfunctorily performed and I did not attempt to study. I noticed that once again the voice of the stone had subsided to a quiet murmur that I could not hear, and I wondered if it would again change the rhyme.

The next morning I again put the stone in the sunlight, and when I heard its voice this time, it was stronger and clearer.

"Wise Child, I shall come to thee
Over land and hill and sea.
Briefly shall my footsteps roam
To take the road that leads you home."

I had the strangest feeling that this was what the stone had been saying all along, but that somehow I had misheard it before. As I made out the words, I cried aloud, "Mother, Mother!"

The voice of the stone grew quiet again in the evening, as I had come to expect, but I was anything but quiet. I felt feverish, unable to sit still or to concentrate on anything. I was like someone tormented by an illness for whom the time passes as slowly as a snail. I lived now for the stone. I awaited its daily proclamation as inevitably as I waited for the sun itself.

The next day the rhyme had changed again.

"I shall make my way to thee—
Ford the river, cross the sea.
The curling wave shall bear you home,
Never ever thence to roam."

As I heard this I had a vision of Maeve setting forth, probably on horseback, with a servant or two, perhaps the man on the black horse who had pursued me. How long would it take her to get to the white house? A day and a night, perhaps, if the tides were right and a ship was crossing. But did the words mean that she had already set off or only that she was thinking about it? Was there a hint of menace in the last line? Why never ever to roam? I had thought that Maeve and I would travel together.

I waited in agony for the next day's words, but my agony was no less when I heard them.

> *"Wise Child, I am on the wave,*
> *Coming thence my child to save.*
> *Loving heart shall bear her home,*
> *Never ever thence to roam."*

I felt stricken as I listened to this, not joyful anymore. I knew that somehow, I did not know how, I had summoned Maeve, and that having summoned her, I did not want her to come, still less to carry me away. I did want her to love me, and I was tempted by the wonders of her luxurious house—the dresses and the books and Bran—but I wanted to be as free as I had been with Juniper, free to learn, to travel, to marry or not marry, to become a *doran* or not. Now Maeve would come and take me away, and I had a feeling that this time she would never let me return to Juniper.

Like someone who has been bitten by a snake, I leaped up from the steps, dropping the stone, and I dashed into the house. I locked the door that was never locked. I gave Daisy an enormous helping of hay and the chickens huge helpings of grain and water. Then I went in and bolted the back door of the house. If Maeve *had* been on the sea that very morning, I calculated she would come ashore sometime that afternoon and would probably reach the house by nightfall.

I sat down in Juniper's chair, and I could feel my heart thumping in terror. As if settling myself for a long vigil, I decided that I needed the bearskin, and I fetched it, wrapped it around my shoulders, and sat down again in Juniper's chair. I felt very alert, as if every part of my body and mind was looking out for signals of Maeve's approach. After a while, when nothing happened, this first terrified state abated a bit. It was still morning and Maeve would not reach me until afternoon. Unless . . . my skin prickled . . . she adopted some other means of travel. If she could do that, I reflected, then locked doors would not keep her out.

The morning wore on, sometimes going very slowly, sometimes galloping past. I could not bear to do anything that needed concentration—the return to reality would be too painful—yet I was bored at the same time as being very frightened. Once or twice I whimpered under the bearskin. The sides of Juniper's chair held me curled up inside it like a pea in a pod. In spite of my fear I eventually became hungry—I had had no breakfast—and I uncurled myself and ate some bread and honey. The familiar food was comforting. This nightmare with Maeve could not be happening. The real world was the world of life with Juniper— books and herbs and stories and laughing together.

Back in the chair again I dozed off. For a long time I tried to fight the sleepy feeling, but gradually it overcame me like a spell. I thought later that I had probably slept for an hour when I heard a small noise outside. At once I was fully alert. Then there was a loud knock on the door.

I had no idea what to do. I could not possibly answer the knock. Even if it did not appear to be Maeve herself, it might be her in disguise, like the stepmother in the fairy tale. How would I know? She would give me something like a red apple—I would take a bite—and then . . . I sat frozen in the chair.

The caller knocked again, even more loudly and firmly

this time. I wanted to shout out, "Go away," but thought it was better to pretend I was not at home.

Just as I was thinking this, something really terrifying happened. There was a sort of scrabbling sound under the window, and then to my horror a face appeared there, nose flattened against the glass. I screamed and put my head under the bearskin.

18

Juniper's Return

THE CALLER was Colman. When I recognized him, I flew to the door to let him in. He looked at me strangely.

"What on earth's the matter with you? Where's Juniper?"

I pulled him in and locked the door behind him.

"You look awful," he said.

Quickly, my eyes filling with tears, I told him the story of the stone and of Maeve.

"Where is the stone?"

"Out on the steps."

"I want to listen to it."

"But Maeve might get in!" I wailed.

"You can see anyone coming up the cliff path at least a hundred yards away," he pointed out. "Plenty of time to get back in and lock the door."

I allowed him to go out and pick up the stone, while I watched nervously from inside. I would not let him bring the stone back in, so he stood there holding it to his ear. I knew that the stone was working—I could hear its murmurs and hissing sibilants even from where I stood.

After holding it to his ear for a minute or two, he looked at me blankly. "Nothing. I can hear nothing," he said. He came back into the house, locked the door carefully behind him, and sat down. I could see that he was struggling with different orders of thought.

"Do you think you could be mistaken?" he asked at last.

"No, no. I heard it. I *heard* it."

"It might be your imagination."

"I *heard* it," I said obstinately again.

AGAIN I FELT some enormous struggle taking place in Colman, a struggle maybe between the scornful small boy who thought I was being silly and the Colman who loved me enough to know that my reality was not necessarily his.

"You could come back home with me," he said doubtfully. We both knew what that meant—explanations to Gregor. Also I had a scared anticipation of a meeting with Maeve on the cliff path.

"I could stay here," he tried again. We both knew what that meant too—a beating from Gregor.

"Colman, would you?"

Colman at once became peacock proud.

"Of course. It's nothing. You can't stay here by yourself."

"I *could*. But I'd rather not."

Having another person there made it all quite different. The two of us lit the fire and started making a meal. We giggled a lot, as we always did, teased each other, talked about Colman's brothers and sisters, about our plans for the future.

At bedtime we curled up in Juniper's big bed together. Somehow the specter of Maeve returned to us as we lay there together in the dark.

"If she has not arrived by now, do you think she is coming at all?" Colman asked me. I knew that he was silently asking me, "Was she ever coming or is the whole thing something like a story in your imagination?"

"I don't know," I said.

"It seems so simple," he said. "You just don't open the door to her, and you stay put until Juniper gets back."

"Bits of me *want* Maeve," I confessed. "Want to believe she loves me. Want to go and be with her."

"Why? You know she doesn't love you. Not like Juniper does, anyway. Besides, you love living with Juniper."

I felt ashamed of the truth—that in part I was still attracted to the life of luxury and ease I believed Maeve would give me, that even though I rather liked the thought of being a *doran,* I was afraid of ending up as a *cailleach* like Juniper, that I did get sick of studying and churning butter and digging peat and cleaning house and milking the cow and harvesting the herbs and learning lines and lines by heart, and all the hundred and one jobs that Juniper seemed to expect. So I repeated only half the truth.

"Bits of me still want Maeve."

"She's not good to you," he said. "My mother says she was cruel to you. When you were a tiny child." As he spoke I felt a pain inside me, and I closed my fingers around the scar on my palm where she . . . I was trying to remember something that I did not want to remember.

"Finbar said you must never live with her anymore. If she was cruel to you once, she might be so again."

"Why would she be?"

"Some people enjoy it. You have to keep out of their way if there's nothing else you can do to stop them."

There was a long silence between us. I was sore and angry with him for what he had just said.

"Mostly when people are called wicked," Colman went on, "they don't seem to be—you know, the sort of people Fillan thinks are wicked. But if there *are* wicked people, I think Maeve might be one of them. I just feel it."

The tears slipped freely down my cheeks onto the pillow. I wanted to shout, "Maeve is my mother!" but I knew that I could not defend her.

Soon Colman fell asleep, so I was left to my painful thoughts. I tossed and turned, tormented by wanting Maeve and not wanting her, by the fear of her arrival, by half memories of a fire that had frightened me, by the dread of cruelty and wickedness. Just as I felt that I could not bear my own mind a moment longer, it was as if someone had touched my burning brow with a cool hand, caressing it; at that very moment came the memory of Juniper's talisman, to which I had never given a thought since Juniper had left. I slipped quietly out of bed, went to the dresser, put my hand under my clothes, and suddenly felt the satiny touch of silver. I heaved a sigh of peace, of relaxation, even as I touched it. I pulled it out and looked at it. I could see it quite clearly in the moonlit room, and I carried it to where the moon's beams rested on it. As if from habit with the stone I lifted it to my cheek, but the talisman sang no song, spoke no rhymes—simply rested in my hand as if it was a perfect fit there. I climbed back into bed still holding it, and fell asleep almost at once.

Presently I woke to Colman standing over me.

"I must go now. Dad may not know I wasn't home with a bit of luck. I'll see you soon."

"Take some bread with you," I said, and went back to sleep.

WHEN I WOKE AGAIN it was sunrise, the eerie half-light of the dawn. I woke because someone out in the garden was calling my name.

"Wise Child, Wise Child . . ."

I knew at once who it was, and I got up unhesitatingly. I went to the window and opened it, and there standing out among the flower beds was Maeve. She was wearing the same clothes she had worn the last time I saw her, and her long, golden-red hair was about her shoulders, though only a ghost of itself in that eerie light, as was Maeve herself. She was holding Bran by his bridle.

To my surprise I no longer felt afraid.

"What do you want?" I asked in a firm voice.

"You summoned me," she said. "Bran and I have come to take you away to the life of a princess and a lady."

"I cannot go anywhere without asking Juniper," I said. "Nor without Finbar's consent."

"Finbar!" she said in a voice of contempt. "He will never return."

"Yes, he will."

"But in any case you summoned me."

"I was wrong to do so. I felt lonely. But I want to live with Juniper."

"Where *is* Juniper? That old enemy of mine."

I did not feel like answering that. It was obvious enough that she wasn't there, but all the same I did not want to say so.

"This is your chance to get away without a fuss. She'd never let you if she was at home. Bran grieves for you."

"I'm not coming."

"Well, at least come out into the garden to greet your mother. Whom you summoned on this long journey."

I could feel the old longing begin to rise in me. More than anything in the world I longed to run down and out into the garden barefooted and in my nightdress and fling myself into Maeve's arms. What stopped me, I think, was a sort of distraction. It was that the talisman in my hand had become burning hot, so hot that I had to hold it gingerly by its edges.

"I cannot come with you or talk with you unless Juniper says I may. If she says it is all right, then I will do it."

Maeve's face seemed to close in on itself.

"We are a good little girl, aren't we?" she said scornfully, and I could feel an old pain stir in me.

"I'm going back to bed now." I shut the window deliberately, padded across the floor to the bed, and got back into it, still clutching the talisman.

The calling began then. To start with I could hear Maeve, out in the garden, calling my name in a high, piercing voice that gradually grew higher and higher, almost like a whistle, until it seemed as if it rang right through my head, rinsing my eardrums with its intolerable sound. Then it was as if the voice was in the room with me—under the bed, up in the high corner of the ceiling, in the middle of the dresser muffled under the clothes, from out of my empty nest, from the window, from the candle stand. I began to tremble violently.

Then the pulling sensations began, as if someone was taking my limbs one by one and stretching them until they went into spasm. I grew very hot, until the perspiration ran down me, and then very cold, until my teeth chattered and I shook as if I was out in a heavy frost. I shook so much that I could hear the legs of the bed rattling on the floor beneath me, a drumming sound that was in itself disturbing and seemed to herald a new and unwelcome stage of torment. The drumming on the floor continued even after I had stopped shaking, and then there was a series of clicks and clucks from all over the room as if the walls, the ceiling, and the furniture were trying to speak to me. Then an extraordinary sense of vertigo seized me. The bed seemed to be spinning on a tiny platform in space, and all around it there was nothing. Sick and terrified, I hid my face, but I could feel the platform tipping, tipping. . . .

Then I was no longer in my room but deep in the underground cavern staring up at that terrible painting of the Devil. But even as I stared, I became part of the painting, the girl held in the dreadful claw, helpless to escape, and the face of the Devil was the face of Maeve.

In that terrible moment time stood still. Then, gradually, the sounds and the sensations died away, and I could see the sky a fresh daffodil yellow outside the window in Juniper's house. I thought I could hear someone shouting in the garden; then there were running steps on the stair, the door flew open, and there was Juniper's beloved face.

"Wise Child . . ." The tone of her voice covered a whole

range of love, concern, understanding, sympathy, sorrow, and knowledge of what I had just gone through.

I DON'T REMEMBER much about the rest of that day, except that a lot of the time I seemed to be sitting on Juniper's lap.

"Colman was here," I said once in a voice like a stranger's. "He stayed the night, but he had to go before . . ." Juniper nodded gravely.

"It was the stone, you see. It kept talking to me. It said that She was coming, and then I got frightened and I bolted all the doors, and then Colman came, and then eventually She did come."

"Yes, she did."

"Colman couldn't hear the stone. He thought I was being silly. . . . I didn't remember about the talisman until last night; then I took it out and held it."

"Where is the stone now?"

"On the front steps, unless Maeve took it."

"How did you get the stone?"

"That first time I saw her . . . before. . . . She gave it to me." My voice faltered, but I continued. "So I brought it home, and because I knew you wouldn't like the idea, I hid it." My voice got fainter. "It was so pretty. At first I forgot all about it, but then I kept taking it out and looking at it, until gradually I couldn't leave it alone."

"I see." As usual Juniper offered neither blame nor rebuke. "My poor Wise Child," and she stroked my hair gently. "And I left you all alone with it—the summoning stone, as it's called."

"People know about it?" It seemed less alarming if it had a name.

"Some people know about it. You see, it gave Maeve power over you, which she wouldn't have had otherwise. Well, not like that."

I knew that I must tell her the hard thing.

"But you see *I* used it to summon *her*. To begin with I really wanted her to come, because I wanted to have an easy life again and ride on Bran and all that. Then Colman said she would be cruel to me . . . and other things . . . and it made it easier to refuse. I could see that I was better off here. So I didn't go."

"*Are* you better off here?" Juniper asked with a hint of a laugh in her voice.

I felt ashamed that with all her love and care for me, I had wanted to run away from her a second time, and I hung my head, so she answered for me.

"I make you work very hard, and sometimes it's boring and you miss other children. And though you would like to be a *doran* sometimes, at other times you don't like the idea at all. I know it's difficult, but I do think it is better for you than living with Maeve, or I'd let you go this very day. Bear with me a few years longer—or at least until Finbar returns—grow bigger and stronger, and all kinds of things might be possible.

"As for Maeve . . . who can say what she intends if she gets you to go to her house . . . but forcing you to do something cannot be right. It is not Finbar's wish that you live with her, and deep down it doesn't seem to be your wish either, or you wouldn't have struggled so hard to stay here."

I was silent for a few moments, humbled by my own folly.

"I like it here," I said. "And I love *you*." And I put my arms around Juniper and kissed her, wondering how I could ever have thought of abandoning her.

"Now we must see what became of the summoning stone, and then we will get some supper," said Juniper, rising. She went out to the steps and then called to me. The stone was still lying where Colman had left it the day before.

"Pick it up, Wise Child. We will take Tillie and go to the Bottomless Lake."

"Must we?" It was several miles to the lake, and I was very tired.

"Yes, we must. You can ride on Tillie."

I picked the stone up unwillingly. The bright colors in it seemed to have gone dead. No sound came from it, only a feeling—what I thought of as a sort of prickle—as if it was punishing me.

"Ouch!"

"Put this cloth round it," said Juniper, as if stones that pricked you were the most normal thing in the world. When we got to the lake she made me take the stone out of its covering—it pricked me again—and throw it out into the middle of the water, where it plopped and sank. I felt better.

"What about all those things she did?" I asked Juniper on the way back. "The noises, and the pulling feelings, and the calling and all that."

"When she puts her mind to it, my darling, your mother is no mean sorceress."

"How did you make her go?" I remembered the raised voices out in the garden.

"I told her to. She was on my ground, you see. Where my power was stronger."

"Wouldn't it be stronger in other places?"

"That would depend."

"Will she come back?"

"Not for a while, I think."

I was silent then, pondering on Juniper's answers. Suddenly, far away across the moor, I could see a running horse.

"Bran!" I gasped. The pony was coming nearer to us but running in great circles like a mad thing. Juniper stood quite still, as if concentrating very hard. I stood beside her, and we must have waited half an hour while Bran galloped around us. Eventually he reached us, but with his eyes rolling and his mouth frothing.

"Don't touch him," Juniper said. As if affected by Juniper's stillness, Bran now stood still, his breath coming in great sobbing heaves. When he had quietened a little, Juniper began saying something in a foreign language. Then, while Bran's head sank lower and lower, she began to walk around him widdershins, signaling me to do the same, all the while reciting. For perhaps an hour she performed this ritual, occasionally making little signs with her hands. Then she approached him and touched his legs, his head, his tail, as if anointing him. When she had finished, he raised his head again and looked at me as if recognizing me for the first time, and I went to him and stroked his face and his neck, which were covered with sweat.

"Poor Bran," said Juniper.

"What was it?" I asked.

"The Evil Eye. But he'll be all right now."

"Can he live with us?" I asked joyfully.

"I think he'll have to," she said. "I can't think what else

we can do with him. It's an ill wind that blows nobody any good," and she gave me one of her wide grins.

Something else was troubling me too.

"The scar on my hand . . ." I mentioned it with difficulty.

I had a clear picture in my head of a room with a great hearth in it, and of myself sitting by the fire, small and frightened because I had done something wrong. Then Maeve, who was as tall as a giantess in my imagining, had picked up the poker, which was still hot from the fire, and struck me with it on the palm of my hand. I had fainted from the pain and had come around alone and terrified.

All this I told Juniper, and she listened in the quiet, dispassionate way she had when you told her something truly terrible. It was as if she was joining things together in her mind, making some act of love and healing where otherwise all was violence and despair. She took my hand and gently unfolded the fingers so that the scar was exposed, and it was as if she took up the whole dreadful incident in her worn, loving hands.

"She didn't love me," I said, the tears pouring down my cheeks.

"I think she did," Juniper replied, "as much as she loved anybody. People who can't show love in any other way sometimes do it by hurting people."

I knew that she was making me a generous gift, the gift of a mother who was not all bad. I sat and considered, the scar that I had always hidden, even from myself, held before me as evidence. I came to a decision.

"From now on," I said, "I choose you to be my mother."

19

The Arrest

THAT WINTER was one of the hardest I can remember. It began with a pervading wetness—continual rain, damp, and mist that went on for weeks—and the wheat and rye and oats, which had stood so fine and tawny under the golden sun of August, began to mildew in the barns. By Christmas the wet had turned to snow, and when lambing time came many of the sheep and their little ones died in the snow, though the men worked till all hours to get to them. What this meant was that our people, never well-fed, would come close to starvation before the spring. In their desperation they would bleed the cattle and mix the blood with their children's food to give them strength, but then the weakened cattle might die or not have the strength to breed healthy stock. As the cruel winter wore on the children grew scrawnier, the mothers more tired-looking, the fathers surlier.

To make matters worse there was rumor of smallpox on the mainland. There had been no smallpox on the island for many years—the unscarred faces of all but the old people showed that it was fifty years since the scourge last came. But everyone was afraid of its return.

IT WAS in the middle of that winter that Colman came one afternoon when he should have been at school. He seemed uneasy, restless, both in his body and in his mind.

We settled in front of the glowing peat fire with a honey drink of Juniper's invention and some oatcakes plastered with butter. Juniper was away looking for some root or leaf, but I knew that there was nothing she liked better than to fill Colman's hungry stomach. Some grunt or grimace of Colman's as we settled on our cushions put an idea into my head.

"Did your dad beat you?" I asked sympathetically. Colman hated it to be mentioned, but I wanted to know.

"Mmm . . . the drink's lovely. I've got something to say. . . ." His honest eyes traveled to my face. "Don't come to our house. And don't come to Mass on Sunday."

He saw the deep hurt on my face and put out a hand to reassure me. "It's not Morag and me and the others. Just Gregor. He's afraid of Fillan Priest."

"But not to come to Mass, though. And not to see the little one anymore . . ." My eyes filled with tears. "Why?"

"It's just for now. It'll blow over. It's just that Fillan says Juniper has bewitched the grain and that she will make the smallpox come."

"That's silly. Why should she do that? And you're my kin. You should stick up for me."

"*I* shan't stop coming, and Morag would come if she dared."

the infection with instructions to take more, baring her sore breasts and holding them thoughtfully in her brown hands, muttering words as if she was addressing them.

I found that nowadays I studied Juniper's methods carefully, imagining what I would do or say in the same situation, learning not so much from the herbs she used as from her whole bearing.

"If we can get this bit right, the little one will feed again and grow strong," Juniper said, and Jean nodded wearily. Slowly the sadness and fear disappeared from her tired face—it was always the same with Juniper's patients, as if her life and energy flowed into them and the intolerable became tolerable. Her eyes closed in sleep and she dozed for perhaps half an hour—I always found these slow, quiet times with Juniper's patients very dull and boring, though Juniper had a way of sitting quite still as if giving them her entire attention even when they were sound asleep. I fed the baby a little of some goat's milk that Juniper had bought from a villager—I watered it, and with a spoon slipped a little into the baby's mouth. At first she wriggled angrily and spat it out, arching her little back with surprising strength, but after a little she took some and seemed able to keep it down.

"Sing to her," said Juniper when the baby had taken a little, and I sat on the floor in front of the feeble fire and sang her a lullaby, as I had often done for my youngest cousin. The baby, as if surprised, opened her wide blue eyes and stared in an unfocused way into my eyes before she fell asleep.

Jean awoke looking as if the fever had left her, and she lay staring quietly before her. Juniper had taken the baby, still wrapped in her shawl, from me and placed her in a basket. She carried her over and laid her beside her mother.

Jean's eyes turned to Juniper's face and the look of fear returned.

"Be careful!" she said urgently. "There's those in this village who would harm you—you know who I mean. Be careful!"

Juniper took her hand.

"Thank you," she said. "I know what you mean and I will take care. And don't be afraid yourself. You need not tell anyone we have been here, you know."

Perhaps it was because I had lived in the village and Juniper had not that I knew it was too late for such caution. Everyone would know that we had seen Jean. As we made our way home along the wet, rutted street, the puddles splashing our clothes, nobody was around to greet us. Under the eaves of two or three of the cottages I noticed bunches of fennel and of rowan hanging.

"What are they for?" I asked Juniper.

"A specific against witches," she said shortly. I wondered if she felt frightened at what Jean had said, but she seemed exactly the same as usual, calm, cheerful, somehow *ordered* inside herself. I pushed the dark fear away from me.

"I am sorry about your shawl," I said. "It was such a lovely color." There was an east wind blowing, and I saw Juniper shiver involuntarily. She did not reply.

AFTER OUR MEAL that night we sat silently by the fireside.

"Colman says that we might be in danger," I said at last. "That I should not go to Mass, nor visit my cousins."

"There is danger," she said. "Or rather, there will be if

the smallpox comes from the mainland. If not . . . then I think we will get through this winter and Fillan can do nothing against me."

"Why does he hate you so much?"

"I think he misunderstands. He thinks that I am working against the new religion, but it is not so. I love and revere Jesus as he does—how could one not? But in the new religion they think that nature, especially in the human body, must be fought and conquered—they seem to fear and distrust matter itself, although in the Mass it is bread and wine that is used to show how spirit and matter are one. They think that those like the *dorans,* who love and cherish nature, must be fought and conquered too. Jesus did not tell them this—it is all their own invention because they fear nature, their own and that of others."

"If the smallpox comes, what will they do to us?"

"I hope you will get away—to Firkeld perhaps—before anything happens. For myself . . . I shall have to wait and see."

"They are . . . cruel . . . to witches sometimes?" I said, not liking to put the idea into words.

"Indeed," said Juniper. "Remember that if you should hear that I have renounced anything, or betrayed anyone."

"You?" I gasped in astonishment. "You could not do that."

"Fear, pain, loneliness, might make anyone say anything," said Juniper. "I hope that I should be brave and strong, but there is no knowing."

"Is this why you want me out of the way?" I said in a sudden flash of grown-up wisdom. "So that at least you need not worry about what they might do to me?"

"That is one reason," she said.

I struggled with this information. I loved Juniper and wanted to stay with her and be brave, as she was, but I was also very frightened at what might happen.

"I just hope the smallpox won't come," I said doggedly.

"Whatever happens, Wise Child, we trust one another to do the best we can. And we love one another. This is a weapon that they cannot take from us. In the end it makes us stronger than they are."

I suddenly realized that Juniper was entirely unafraid. She calculated what they might do to her if the smallpox came, and she measured her own strength as best she could in the hope that she would not betray her friends if they tortured her, but in the core of her she was untouched by the sense of threat, as cheerful and confident as she had always been.

"I do like knowing you," I said, stammering. Really, I was trying to say something much more difficult—that through her, as though through a window, I could see the love that was woven through every fiber of the world.

IN THE DAYS and weeks that followed, the little bunches of herbs that hung in the eaves of people's houses grew more numerous, and the requests for Juniper to visit sick people grew fewer and fewer until they finally stopped altogether. When we met people on the road—men and women whom Juniper had helped and healed—they turned away without speaking to us. Juniper seemed not to mind, but it made me feel very lonely. I no longer visited my cousins, nor became an ordinary villager again for the length of the Mass. Worse than this, however, was the dread that hung over us—the dread that Fillan would work out his old grudge against Juniper in a terrible way. There was nothing we could do but wait—wait for times to get better, for a return to the happy days when Juniper had visited the sick people, for the spring and the time when people would be less hungry. I found it hard to concentrate on anything, to get on with lessons or with preparing herbs for people who no longer wanted Juniper to visit them.

IN SPITE of our waiting, when the blow fell it came as a surprise. I had gone out one day across the bog in search of a plant Juniper needed when, long before I reached home, I saw Cormac in the distance. I think I knew at that very moment that disaster had struck, but I went on quietly until I stood before him. Cormac's face, though scarred, was now very nearly healed.

"They have arrested Juniper," he said simply. "The smallpox has arrived, and Fillan has used it to stir up feeling against her, as we feared. Of course, they are waiting for you at the white house. I think Juniper hoped you might somehow flee to Firkeld, but I do not think you will get so far."

I stood on the track rooted with terror.

"I'm frightened!" I said. At that moment I felt a presentiment that both Juniper and I would be burned as witches. I knew that I had no alternative to being arrested—Fillan would have the ferries to the mainland watched, and I would never get to Firkeld—but I wanted a little more time before I fell into their hands.

"May I come to your hut?" I asked. "Just for an hour or two?"

For most of the day Cormac and I sat together in his hut.

"You know that I would do anything for Juniper," he said, "and for you, too." I took Cormac's hand in gratitude and found comfort in his brown eyes.

"In a way it's a relief it's come," I said. "It was awful waiting, feeling all the people had turned against Juniper."

"They were frightened," he said. "Frightened of Fillan, frightened of the inquisition. Otherwise they would support Juniper, who has cared for them as she cared for me."

"They will let themselves be led like a pack of dogs," I said, quoting Colman.

It was comforting to sit there for a little in the room where I had often sat with Juniper, and to feel that Cormac loved her as much as I did. I sat with my head on my hand, trying to take in the fact that Juniper had been arrested and must even now be being interrogated by the inquisitor, or shut in the tiny prison that usually held drunks. In my mind I sent a message of love to her.

As it grew later, however, I knew that I could not postpone my return any longer. Cormac and I threw our arms around each other in a long, comforting hug and then, slowly, and shrinking inwardly, I made my way to the white house. I approached it through the yard, circled it, and looking through a window into the big room, caught a glimpse of Fillan's sandy head.

20

The Trial

THE FIRST TIME they questioned me was in Fillan's house. I was questioned by both Fillan and the inquisitor from the mainland, an English monk who was called Radmon. He was tall, with piercing eyes, and when we stood together he towered above me. To begin with he was friendly.

"So this is the little girl," he said. I curtsied, as I had always been taught to do. He sat me directly in front of him on a stool. There were only a couple of feet between us, a distance I found uncomfortable, and I moved the stool back a little until my back was against the wall. This achieved nothing, since he instantly moved farther forward. Fillan sat to one side, where I had to turn my head to see him.

"You have lived with Ninnoc, commonly known as Juniper," he began. "For how long?"

"For over a year, sir."

"She clothed and fed you."

"Yes, sir."

"Was she kind to you?"

"Very kind, sir."

"I take it that she expected you to work during that time?"

"She did, sir."

"So what work did you do?"

"I cleaned the house. I made cheese and butter, I ground the meal for our bread, I collected eggs, I milked Daisy, I did a bit of spinning and weaving—not much, because I wasn't very good at it—I—"

"Weaving? What did you weave?"

"Cloth, sir." I sounded as innocent as I knew how. "Cloth for our winter clothes."

"What else did you do?"

"I weeded the garden. I helped dry the herbs, I chopped them up or grated the roots, I helped make ointments and extracts and tinctures, sir."

"And these . . . potions. What were they for?"

"To make people well, sir. To make them better from skin diseases, and dropsy, and milk infection, and rheumatism, and earache, and the baby fever, and winter sickness, and measles."

"Very laudable, I am sure. What about the other uses of these herbs?"

"What other uses, sir?"

"Uses for spells. To make people fall ill instead of better, to give them smallpox, say, or to make their cattle sick, or their crops mildew. Or maybe to make people fall in love?"

"Juniper didn't do things like that, sir. She wanted to help people. She was kind."

There was a long silence between us, and the inquisitor started on another tack.

"You think of yourself as a Christian, child?"

"Of course."

"You go to Mass?"

"I did until lately."

"And what prevented you then?"

"Fillan Priest was saying things about Juniper."

"So Juniper would not let you go?"

"I did not want to hear him say things like that."

"You know that you were very wrong to cut yourself off from the source of grace?"

I did not answer, and he said at length, "Well?"

"If you say so, sir."

"But you don't agree with me?"

"I am glad of the grace, sir, but I do not like to hear Juniper criticized."

"Very well. But you would agree that Juniper is not a Christian?"

"I do not know, sir."

"She did not go to Mass, did she?"

"No, sir. But she spoke well of the Lord, and told me to emulate him."

The inquisitor's eyelids flickered, I thought, with annoyance.

"Did she ever speak of another Lord?"

"What other Lord, sir?"

"Of another Lord whom she worshiped?"

"No, sir."

"Fillan tells me that she gave you lessons. In what subjects?"

"Latin. English. The language they speak in Cornwall and in Brittany. Poetry. Philosophy. Astronomy. Mathematics, especially geometry. Herbal lore."

"Spells?"

"No, no spells, sir. I once taught her a spell, a charm really, that a boy in the village had taught me for the toothache, and she thought it very funny."

The inquisitor moved a little restlessly on his chair, and I guessed that whereas he had begun by thinking a little girl would be easy to question, he had started to think it might be more difficult. I felt a tiny bit triumphant, though I knew I must be on my guard.

"That will do for now," he said to Fillan. "Keep her locked up, and I will question her again tomorrow."

As I rose thankfully to my feet and began to cross the room to the door, he threw a sudden question at me.

"Did you ever see Juniper fly?"

"Never, sir," I said truthfully.

I spent that night locked in a room in Fillan's house. If I craned my neck out of the window I could see the lockup where Juniper must be kept. I sent a message to her in my mind, and it seemed as if a message of love came back from her. I was tired, and I slept well—as if I was refusing to think about being a prisoner for the time being. When I next saw the inquisitor—about nine in the morning—I felt rosy and well. By concentrating on each moment as it happened—something I suddenly realized I had learned from Juniper—I could keep myself from gnawing anxiety.

Today the inquisitor talked to me by himself, and he took a different tack.

"You must love Juniper very much?" he said.

I was so surprised by this that I did not reply immediately. Finally I said, "She has been very good to
me, sir."

"You were very lucky that she took you in and cared for
you when you were homeless?"

"It was what Finbar wanted," I said primly.

"Quite so. But to find yourself in a good home, with
plenty to eat, that was lucky, was it not?"

I did not answer, though I was not sure why. I did not
trust him.

"She treated you well, did she not, so you must love her
very much?"

My face set into one of its obstinate, sulky looks. He
could never know of the life between me and Juniper—of
the laughter and the gentleness, of the times I had sat on her
lap, the times she had sung to me and told me stories, and
taught me things my hungry mind wanted to know. What
did all that have to do with this huge monk? I knew only
that he wanted to hurt Juniper.

The questioning went on for most of that day, with
breaks for meals. He asked who Juniper's friends were,
where she went on her travels, whether I had ever visited the
caves under the white house, whether I had been to ceremonies with her in which we worshiped the Devil. I pretended to have forgotten the names of her friends, or not to
have known them, and the other questions I could reply
truthfully to.

"Is it true that she would not let you return to your
natural mother?" the inquisitor asked. Reaching through
the strands of our long conversation I detected, with a stirring of dread, the presence of Maeve.

"She may be my mother, but she is not a good person,"
I said, sounding very proper. "She is not kind, nor a Christian, and I prefer to live with Juniper."

At last the long day came to a close. I was locked in my
bedroom, and I could hear Fillan and the inquisitor talking
and laughing down below as they ate their dinner. I was
tired, but now it was hard to sleep—I kept going over and
over the conversation to make sure that I had said nothing
that could harm Juniper. I got out of bed more than once to
look at the little jail and to try to commune with Juniper.
I took the talisman and held it in my hand as I tried to go
to sleep. When at last I did sleep, I had bad dreams, and I
was brusquely awakened by Fillan shaking me.

"The inquisitor wants to talk to you."

I threw a blanket around my shift and descended barefoot
to the living room. The fire had died down, and I felt very
cold. With a painful shock I realized that I had left the
talisman behind in the bedroom.

"Juniper's friends?" the inquisitor began. "What are their
names?"

"I never knew their proper names."

"They were known by titles? What sort of titles? Tell us
one or two of them."

"They were known by nicknames—as I am, and as Juniper is."

"What nicknames?"

I rapidly invented one or two names.

"The child has not taken an oath," Fillan interrupted at
this point. "She is old enough to do so."

A Bible was brought, and I was made to swear upon it.

"You understand, child," Fillan said to me. "If you say

with him—his grave, sweet expression was immensely comforting at a moment when I needed comfort.

Juniper came in from the side entrance of the church. She was thin and drawn-looking, but her eyes were alight, she moved easily, and when I dared to look at her, she smiled at me as lovingly as ever. Did she not know the use they had put me to?

The inquisitor started gently, politely—it struck me that he was trying to get the people onto his side.

"Your name is Ninnoc, commonly known as Juniper."

"Yes."

"It is alleged that you are guilty of acts of witchcraft— that you did bring murrain upon the corn of one Dugald of this village, that you did bewitch one Fingal so that he believed himself in love, that you did afflict one Gill with the smallpox. . . ." (So smallpox *had* reached the village at last.) Juniper again briefly exchanged glances with me, and with the movement of an eyelid so faint that no one but me would have known what it was, I knew that she had winked at me. I cheered up at once, sat up straighter, determined that somehow or other she and I would survive this experience or at any rate die with what dignity we could manage.

Radmon began calling witnesses to make the case against Juniper. Dugald came first. He was one whom Juniper had once described to me as "Fillan's dog." Dugald haunted the church, was always at Mass, praying loudly, always agreed with every word Fillan spoke. It was not difficult to guess how he had been persuaded to give evidence. Fingal was a poor creature who had once asked Juniper's advice about why no woman loved him. He had wanted her to give him a potion that he could put into the drink of Margaret, the girl he fancied. Juniper had said that that was no good—that people must love you of their own accord or not at all. As for Gill—no one seemed able to prove how Juniper might have given him the smallpox. It struck me that apart from my evidence, there was little on which to convict her. Obviously, through God knew what suffering, she had refused to "confess."

IT WAS MY TURN to speak at last, and trembling, I swore on the Bible to be truthful.

"You have for the last year and a half lived at the house of Ninnoc?"

"Yes."

"I want you to tell the court how during that time Juniper has educated you."

"She has taught me Latin and English and other languages, mathematics and astronomy, poetry and singing, playing the harp and herbal lore."

"And what else?"

"How do you mean?"

"She has taught you all these things for one purpose, has she not?"

"To make me learned," I said, obstinately stupid.

"Learned for what purpose?"

"Because she thinks girls should be educated just as boys are."

"That was not what you said when you were interviewed. You will remember that what you said was that Juniper educated you in this way so that you might become a *doran*. Now, remembering that you are speaking upon oath, will you please answer? Did you, or did you not, say that you were pursuing this course of learning in order to become a *doran*?"

I murmured an inaudible reply.

"Will you please speak louder. We cannot hear you. Did you, or did you not . . . ?"

"Yes," I said, turning very red.

"Not everyone is familiar with the vocabulary of witchcraft. Perhaps you will tell us now what a *doran* is."

"It is someone who loves all the creatures of the world," I said, "the animals, birds, plants, trees, and people, and who cannot bear to do any of them any harm. It is someone who believes that they are all linked together and that therefore everything can be used to heal the pain and suffering of the world. It is someone who does not hate anybody and who is not frightened of anyone or anything."

I could see from the expression on the inquisitor's face that he had not expected such a reply. As I had spoken, a murmuring had arisen from among the people, as if my words had brought back recollection of the life of Juniper among them. To tell you the truth, the words surprised me, too. I did not know that I thought all that until I started to say it—I simply remembered how Juniper had seemed to me.

The inquisitor took refuge in sarcasm.

"The little girl learned her lesson well," he said, but after that he told me to sit down. He gave a long speech in which he painted a picture of me as a small pitiful child in the clutches of a powerful witch. Despite my recent ordeals, I knew that I looked well and made a poor argument for him.

Dugald's evidence was spiteful. He remembered seeing

Juniper in the road outside his barn pointing with a bone. That very afternoon he had discovered that the crop was ruined.

Fingal, when he spoke, seemed uneasy, as if he could not remember the course of events too clearly. He contradicted himself, and at one point said that Juniper had said that people must love of their own accord. (His argument had originally been that Juniper had somehow compelled him to love Margaret.) Many people in the village, I reckoned, must have shared their passionate longings with Juniper and been given the same advice. Juniper thought that it was mainly luck whether someone loved you in return, and if they didn't it was no good grieving over it.

At the end of the first day of Juniper's trial all the witnesses had spoken, but Juniper herself had not done so. Tomorrow, after she had, the inquisitor would sum up. If he found her guilty, he would give her a day to repent. She would die whether or not she repented—only repentance made the manner of death less horrible.

Alone in my room I wept over Juniper, sad and guilty at having betrayed her. I wept for myself, too. With her gone, what would become of me? What might they do to me? Where would I live? I took out the talisman from its hiding place and clutched it in my hand, and at once I knew something with complete certainty. I must get out of that room and seek help for Juniper, even though I could not imagine where it would come from. Yet the only way out of the room was to climb down to the street, and it was a long, dangerous way down, so dangerous that it never occurred to my captors that I might attempt it. I pushed the window open and leaned out, and felt dizzy simply looking and sick as I thought of the danger. What I had to do was climb out on the window sill, and edge my way along a piece of timber to the next window and from there to a lower roof at right angles. Then I must walk up that roof and down the other side, move to a lower roof and thence by Iain's cottage to the street.

Even as I thought this, I saw Fillan and the monk leave the house and walk away. It was nearly dark, so if I climbed out no one would see me. While I waited for the darkness, I put on my cloak but pushed it back from my shoulders to leave my arms free. My hands trembling slightly, I put the talisman safely in my pocket. With that perhaps I would not fall.

Being out on the window sill frightened me enough by itself. Foolishly I looked down, and for a few moments became so transfixed with fear that I almost climbed in again. But I looked down the street to the jail where Juniper was kept, and this along with the memory of the day by the stream and my shame at what I had said gave me strength to continue. As I moved across the second window, I simply prayed that Fillan's servant would not be within—I dared not look. When I got to the roof, I remembered what Colman had once told me about roofs—that you walked on them with the outside of one foot and the inside of the other and that you pretended you were going up a hill. Without pausing to think, but aware of the warmth of the talisman in my pocket, I walked up one side of the roof and down the other. I was so exhilarated by my own cleverness that my foot very nearly slipped as I got to the top. I sat for a moment on the ridge of the roof, scarcely able to believe my own courage; then I swung a leg over and began the more difficult journey downward. As I bumped and slid toward the ground I realized with horror that there were voices just beneath me, talking inside the cottage. I was obliged to jump from the low roof and was fearful of the noise I would make. As I hit the ground I almost groaned aloud from the pain in my feet, but the people in the cottage were talking so loudly that they did not hear me. Moving quietly, I opened the gate of their garden and slid out into an alley at the back. Five minutes later I was making my birdcall outside Colman's house, and soon he joined me in our secret place.

21

The Ship

COLMAN DID NOT seem at all surprised to see me. "I thought you might get out," he said. "I was waiting for you."

In the long hours of sitting in the church listening to the trial, Colman had hatched a plan. Donal, the jailkeeper, was also the village shoemaker. Colman would go to see him and ask him to make him a pair of shoes. The keys of the jail, everyone knew, were kept hanging on nails inside Donal's front door—since no one ever tried to get anyone out of our tiny prison (most of the people confined in it were men so drunk that they were left there overnight to sober up), it would not occur to him to hide them. Somehow Colman would distract Donal's attention and then go to the jail and let Juniper out.

The really difficult part came after that. If Juniper and I headed for the eastern coast of the island and tried to get to the mainland, we would be overtaken and recaptured. Where could we go?

Naturally our first thought was the warren of tunnels in the cliff. We could certainly hide there. So far they had not discovered the door behind the table and the wall hanging, and even if they did so, we might still elude them since Juniper knew secrets of the caves that they did not. But the problems were still daunting. What would we eat, and how would we get fresh supplies of food? However, the choice between alternatives still seemed to me a simple one.

"If we leave Juniper where she is," I said, "they will torture and kill her. This way at least there is a chance. You and Cormac might be able to smuggle some food in to us, and eventually, if they think she has vanished, they will stop looking for her and we can go to the coast."

We arranged that Colman would set off at once on his errand to Donal, and that I would wait hidden near the rock that led into the tunnel. By a circuitous route I passed across the road that led into the village and edged my way along the cliff until I found the rock. I sat down to wait.

It was several hours, hours in which I was cold, miserable, and frightened, before my sharp ears caught the rustling in the bushes that meant Colman was on his way back. He gave the curlew cry to warn me of his arrival, and I ran through the trees and low scrub to embrace Juniper. Even in the darkness I could feel her cheerfulness and calm, as if all of us were engaged upon some delightful adventure instead of fighting for our lives.

"We must go," she said.

"Go?"

"Across the island to the west." The west led only to a rocky deserted coast, and I could not imagine any good reason for going there.

"Why?"

"You'll see. It'll be safer than the caves. We might easily starve there."

But I could see no good reason to go westward. Often in the past Juniper had seemed to know about things before they happened, but they had been small, ordinary things, not things upon which our lives depended. What did I really believe about her power? Was it only good for curing measles and the milk infection, or did it extend far beyond that? I wished I knew.

Suddenly I felt terrible again. I was tired, and hungry, and now, in the middle of the night, I must begin the long walk across the island.

"All right," I said. "Coming, Colman?"

"No," he said. "I want to see what happens here."

"Won't they guess you helped me escape?" said Juniper. "It will be dangerous for you to remain."

Colman's face set in obstinate lines.

She did not argue with him.

"All right. Let's go," she said to me.

I STILL do not care to remember that journey. Neither Juniper nor I had slept the previous night, and we had many weary miles to walk on a journey that started by climbing a sheer cliff. It was morning before we had reached the top of the cliff and set off across country, and exhausted as we were, we felt that we must keep going across the great moor, putting as many miles as possible between ourselves and the village. Colman had thoughtfully given us a loaf of bread, but it was the only food we would have for several days, so we did not dare eat too much of it. We drank some water from a stream and lay down for the night on some stones, but it was so bitterly cold that we alternately lay huddled together for warmth or walked up and down. Far from rested, and desperately anxious about pursuit, we set off again early the next morning.

Juniper was very pale and silent, but at moments her old gaiety would flash out. Our problem was beginning to be sheer physical weakness. The journey was perhaps only forty miles or so from start to finish, but hungry and tired as we were, it seemed much farther. The second day in particular seemed to drag on forever, my mind playing tricks with time so that one moment I would imagine we were nearly at the end of our journey and the next that we had only just begun it. When one or the other of us was feeling stronger, she would sing or tell a story to keep up the spirits of the other, trying to make it bearable to keep our weary legs moving.

"There was a princess," Juniper would say, "who was so cross and ugly that she had no suitors at all, although she was the heiress to vast estates. . . ." For a little while I would forget my troubles.

"All this will be good to look back upon," Juniper said once, and I fervently wished that I was already looking back upon it from some safe and comfortable situation, rested and well-fed.

The second night was worse than the first, because it began to drizzle.

"What will happen when we get to the coast?" I asked Juniper.

"I don't know," she replied. It was not a reassuring answer.

"So why are we going, then?" I longed for a crumb of comfort.

"Because it feels right," she said. I could not think of another question, but decided at that point that Juniper might be a little mad, and that probably there was no hope for us. We would get to the coast, and there we would be trapped until Fillan's men came and caught us.

Next morning we set off limping, unable to imagine that we could finish the journey. By now we had our arms around each other's waists, each helping the other along, encouraging, supporting when, as often happened, one or the other of us stumbled from fatigue. Suddenly, away in the distance, we caught a glimpse of distant islands and of the sea, and we broke into a ragged cheer.

All of this while we had often looked behind us during the daylight hours, scouring the bleak moorland for signs of pursuers. In the brief hours of sleeping we had dreamed of capture.

As we used the last of our strength to breast a shallow hill, I turned, the way I had done often before on this flight, and away on the hillside behind us I could distinctly see three figures silhouetted against the sky, one tall, one medium-size, and one small. Behind them, I guessed, still out of sight beneath the brow of the hill, there might be many more. I kept silent. If disaster had overtaken us at last, I could not bear to know it.

Now at last we were standing on the cliffs, with the sea at our feet and a splendid landscape of islands before us, the one that looks like a ship and the one that looks flat like a hat. There, right in the middle of the bay, with the sun shining on it was a real ship, a big ship with a striped sail.

For a moment I searched in my mind for the place where I had seen that great sail and the fine black hull before, and then it came to me.

"It's *The Holy Trinity!*" I shouted at Juniper. "Finbar's ship!"

She nodded with a look of peculiar pleasure and modesty all at once, so that I should not think she was thinking, *I told you so.*

We scrambled down a rough track to the beach, stumbling, falling, and sliding. Already a new problem had arisen. The *Trinity* was anchored a long way out. How should we draw its attention to us? I remembered the men on the hillside behind us, perhaps an hour away from us. If Finbar was to rescue us, then we must waste no time.

We shouted. Juniper took off her white underskirt, put it on a stick, and waved it. I hunted for driftwood and then tried desperately, and hopelessly, by rubbing stones together, to make the spark that would light a fire. No response came from the ship. It was still early morning, and for all we could tell everyone on the vessel was asleep, deaf to our cries. Eventually we sat down exhausted, our brief spell of energy spent now that no answer came from the *Trinity.* It seemed the moment to tell Juniper of what I had seen on the hillside, and sadly, heavily, I did so. She nodded.

More from instinct than from any hope that we would escape detection there, we used the last of our strength to scramble into a cave high in the cliff wall above the beach. Here at least we could watch the *Trinity* for signs of life, could continue to hope till the last moment.

"If Finbar only knew I was here," I said sadly. I felt a

great surge of love for Juniper, who had cared for me and whom Fillan would destroy.

"I love you, Juniper," I said, so that there should be no mistake.

"I know," she said. "I love you, Wise Child."

So DEEPLY was I into the sad feeling of being trapped because we could not tell the *Trinity* we were there that I did not at first notice the extraordinary sound from the cliff overhead. There, quite distinctly, was the cry of a curlew, repeated three times.

To the surprise of Juniper, who knew nothing of our secret call, I leaped up and tore out of the cave, tumbling down the beach so that I could look up. There, many feet above me, stood the figures of three people: Colman, Cormac, and . . . a tall, sunburned figure with hair as black as my own and a great beard. With an extraordinary sense of joy and recognition, of dizzy happiness and shaky wonder, I realized that I was looking at Finbar.

It was much later, when we were safely on the ship, that I asked Juniper again why she had gone west across the island. Had she known Finbar would be there?

"Not exactly," she said. "I just knew that it would be the right thing to do. Most of the time. Once or twice, walking across the island, I thought that I might have made a ghastly mistake, or even be quite mad, but on the whole I thought it would be all right." And she laughed.

"Did you use magic?" I asked her.

"My sort of magic," she said. "The kind that depends on things fitting together." This left me puzzled and rather disappointed, as if maybe our rescue had been little more than a matter of luck. Probably she didn't have much power after all, dearly as I loved her.

As we sailed out of the bay, Juniper and I stood together in the prow of the ship. Somewhere behind us on the deck, giving orders to his men, was Finbar, a bearded stranger of whom I felt quite shy, and whom I would now have to get to know all over again. My world seemed to have changed, and I no longer knew where I was, or who I was. The sun was slowly going down, making the whole world golden, when I saw it.

"Look," I said to Juniper. "Look there!" Ahead of us in the sea, clear as clear, was Tir-nan-Og, the magic island of the west. Serene in amethyst and lapis, in pearl and coral and jade, were the palaces of the unearthly kingdom.

"Manannan has drawn his cloak back so that we can see it. Oh, Juniper, isn't it beautiful?" I turned to look at her and saw, not my own familiar Juniper, but a woman crowned and glorious, beautiful and strong, a magician at the height of her powers. At that moment I knew, beyond a shadow of doubt, that I, Wise Child, should become a *doran*.

MONICA FURLONG is best known in the United States for her two award-winning books for young adults, *Wise Child* and its prequel, *Juniper*. In her homeland of England, Monica was many things—journalist, biographer, novelist, feminist, activist, and social commentator and critic. To all of these roles, Monica brought her abiding commitment to the Christian faith and her simultaneous disillusionment with established social structures. Confronting injustice and hypocrisy wherever she found it, Monica campaigned for changes to laws that discriminated against homosexuals and successfully led a movement for the ordination of women in the Church of England.

Monica Furlong finished *Colman,* the sequel to *Wise Child,* just before her death in January 2003 in Devon, England. She was seventy-two years old.

DISCARD

J FURLONG
Furlong, Monica.
Wise Child /

PEACHTREE

OCT 15 2004

Atlanta-Fulton Public Library